Conversations in Another Room

Conversations
in Another Room
— A Novel

GABRIEL JOSIPOVICI

METHUEN

First published in Great Britain 1984
by Methuen London Ltd
11 New Fetter Lane, London EC4P 4EE
Copyright © 1984 Gabriel Josipovici
Printed in Great Britain by
Richard Clay (The Chaucer Press) Ltd,
Bungay, Suffolk

British Library Cataloguing in Publication Data

Josipovici, Gabriel
    Conversations in another room.
    I. Title
    823'.914 [F]   PR6060.064

    ISBN 0-413-55930-0

For Rosalind Belben

She said: 'Rejoice, for God has brought you to your fiftieth year in the world!' But she had no inkling that, for my part, there is no difference at all between my own days which have gone by and the distant days of Noah about which I have heard. I have nothing in the world but the hour in which I am: it pauses for a moment, and then, like a cloud, moves on.

Samuel Hanagid, 993–1056

I

The niece arrives at the same time every Saturday morning. She stands on the landing smiling, laughing, the big straw hat flapping as she does so. But once she is inside the flat she disappears straight into the old lady's room.

In the spring and summer she carries a bunch of flowers. Two, sometimes, one for the old lady and one for her companion. Things she has picked herself in her garden, with long ferns and other kinds of leaves in the midst of wild roses and fuchsias and nasturtiums. Sometimes she also brings a pretty plate or a teapot she has picked up in a junk shop, slightly cracked or even, when one examines it carefully, chipped. She is a great accumulator, a great giver.

— I don't need all this stuff, the old lady says at once, whatever it is the niece takes out of her big raffia bag and puts on the table beside her bed.

— You'll find a place for it, Phoebe, the niece says. She sits in the upright armchair that is always drawn up at the head of the bed; sometimes she keeps her straw hat on, sometimes she takes it off and lays it on the floor under her chair. Whatever she does Phoebe recounts in detail to her companion afterwards:

— For the first ten minutes she kept her hat on. Then she took it off and put it under her chair.

— Why for ten minutes? the companion asks.

— How should I know? Phoebe says. She just did.

— Her cold seemed better, the companion says.

— No, it wasn't, Phoebe says. It was as bad as ever. I don't like to tell her but I wonder if it's an idea her coming to see an old lady like me with such a cold.

— I thought it was better, the companion says. I didn't hear her sneezing the way she did last week.

— You're growing deaf, Phoebe says.

— Perhaps, the companion says. Though I don't think so.

But now, as the girl puts the plate, or it might be the teapot, on the little bedside table for her aunt to admire, and next to it the bunch of freshly picked flowers, Phoebe says:

— I don't need all this stuff. What shall I do with it?

— You'll find a place for it, Phoebe, the girl says.

— What shall I do with it at my age? the old lady says.

— What has age got to do with it? the girl asks. And you're not as old as all that anyway.

— I don't like the smell of flowers and I don't like the look of flowers, the old lady says. They make a mess.

— Oh but you *must* like them, the niece says. You can't not like them.

— I don't see why not, the old lady says.

— It's just not natural, the niece says.

— Humpf, the old lady says.

— I'll give them to Mary, the niece says.

— What for?

— She can put them in her room, the niece says. I know she appreciates them.

— Humpf, the old lady says again.

– She can put some in the hall, the niece says.

– What for?

– What for? the niece says. Well, it makes the place look bright. Cheerful.

– You think Mary wants to make anything look bright and cheerful? the old lady asks.

– Oh, Phoebe! the niece says.

Then they both laugh.

– Thank you all the same, the old lady says.

– I like giving you things, the niece says. You don't want to deprive me of that pleasure, do you?

– No, dear, the old lady says. You keep right on doing it. But you don't want to deprive me of the pleasure of grumbling either, do you?

Recently the niece has taken to arriving with a man in tow. He is a big, broad-shouldered young man with thick straight black hair which keeps falling over his face.

– This is Mike, she announces. He does not seem particularly interested. He stands on the landing, towering over her, unsmiling. When he enters the flat he has to bend just a little at the door.

The first time she brings him along she takes him straight in to the old lady to introduce him. She explains that he drives her here and it's easier like that.

– What am I supposed to do? the old lady asks her.

– Oh, Phoebe! the girl says. Be nice to him, that's all.

– I have nothing against him, the old lady says. I don't know him. How can I be other than nice to him? His size is rather against him though, she adds.

– She's only teasing, the girl reassures him.

But the old lady has made up her mind. Over most things she makes up her mind at once. There are very few things she cannot make up her mind about. And then they worry her. And she won't let them alone. And comes back to them, again and again. Partly, it's age. Partly, other things.

— He can sit in the hall, she says.

— In the hall? the niece says.

— There's a perfectly comfortable chair there, the old lady says. Like that he doesn't need to pretend to pay attention to things which can be of no possible interest to him.

— Well, the niece says doubtfully, I suppose that's all right.

So now he sits in the hall, waiting for the girl to finish with her aunt. He does not seem to mind. He crosses his legs and stares at the toe of his well-polished light brown shoe. He wears the new type of shoe, called Kickers, with thick soles and a little red tag on the shoe of the left foot, next to the laces, and a little green tag on the shoe of the right foot.

— Is that so that he can remember which is which? the old lady asks.

— Oh, Phoebe! the girl says. It's port and starboard.

— Port and starboard? the old lady says.

— So they told him at the shop, the girl says.

— What nonsense! the old lady says. Port and starboard is boats.

— Apparently it's shoes as well, the girl says.

— You can't have heard properly, the old lady says.

Sometimes the man takes a notebook out of one of the pockets of his jacket and a pen out of another, and writes, leaning the notebook on his knee or on the wooden arm of the chair. When he writes he does not look up. He bites his lower lip, passes his tongue over his upper lip or tugs at the mesh of his hair which keeps falling down over his forehead.

The convex mirror hangs over him as he sits a little to the right of the front door. In it the top of his head can be seen, and the nape of his neck, the hall itself, the door to the old lady's bedroom and the corridor leading to the rest of the flat. It is impossible to make out what he is writing, though the pages of the little notebook shine white in the mirror. By looking very hard it is just possible, in the mirror, to see along the corridor, to two further doors, one of which is usually closed, the other ajar.

— Well, who is he? the old lady asks as soon as he has left the room and the door has closed behind him.

— A friend, the niece says.

— Have you talked to me about him before? the old lady asks.

— I'm not sure. Probably.

— I don't remember your ever mentioning him, the old lady says.

— Oh? the niece says.

— And I remember everything, you know, the old lady says. There's nothing I don't remember.

She lies quite motionless in the large bed, propped on four pillows, staring straight ahead of her, not looking at the girl. When the door is open into the hall it is possible to see her like that, reflected in the convex mirror.

— And so I should, the old lady says. I have nothing to do, you know.

The girl plays with the ribbon on her straw hat.

— I have an almost perfect memory, the old lady says.

And I have no recollection of your ever mentioning him.

— Then I can't have, can I? the niece says, and laughs. She has a light, tinkling laugh which bursts out of her unexpectedly, like the breath of someone who is suddenly thumped on the back.

— What is he in your life? the old lady wants to know.

— I told you, Phoebe, the niece says. He drives me here.

— He's your chauffeur?

The girl laughs. Sometimes, when she laughs, the glasses in the corner cupboard tinkle too.

— Oh, Phoebe!

— Isn't that what they're called?

— He's not a chauffeur! the niece says. Can you imagine me having a chauffeur, Phoebe?

— Of course I can, the old lady says. In my day everyone had chauffeurs. But of course cars were a lot more dangerous then. Not everyone could handle them. I'm told now they're not really much more difficult to control than tricycles.

— He's a friend, the niece says.

— If he's a friend why haven't you mentioned him before?

— I'm sure I have, the niece says.

— If you had I'd have remembered, the old lady says. I wouldn't have been surprised the way I have been.

— You didn't look surprised, the niece says.

— I may have lost some of my wits, the old lady says, but I hope I haven't lost my manners.

Now the girl always arrives accompanied by the man. As soon as the door closes behind her he sits down on the chair in the hall and crosses his legs and stares at the polished toe of his funny shoe. Sometimes he takes out his notebook and pencil and writes, head bowed, without looking up. Occasionally he stops, sucks his pen and stares vaguely ahead of him. He is not looking at anything when he does this, not at anything in the hall. His eyes are blank. He seems to be trying to work something out in his head.

At first the niece would just bring him in to say hello to the old lady, but one day, when the door had shut behind him, the old lady said:

– I don't think that's necessary, do you?

– What, Phoebe?

– To bring him in just to say hello.

– You don't want to see him?

– No, the old lady says. I don't particularly. And he doesn't either.

– I'm sorry, the girl says.

– I'm not, the old lady says.

– I'm sorry if it's inconvenient for you.

– Oh I don't mind him sitting in the hall, the old lady says. If he's *useful* to you.

– He's very kind, the niece says.

– Is he? the old lady says.

– Not everyone would give up their Saturdays just to drive me here, the niece says.

– Well then it's a kindness to spare him the sight of me, the old lady says.

– Oh, Phoebe! the girl says.

– And a kindness to me to spare me the sight of him, the old lady can't help adding.

At eleven o'clock sharp the companion is in the habit of bringing a cup of coffee for the girl and a glass of fruit-juice for the old lady. The man always refuses both.

– Thank you, Mary, the old lady says. That will be all. The companion hovers near the door.

– Thank you, Mary, the old lady says. She waits in silence for the companion to depart and shut the door behind her.

The old lady sighs and sips the fruit-juice. The girl is silent, looking into her cup.

– Do you live together? the old lady wants to know.

– Phoebe! the niece says, blushing. One doesn't ask questions like that.

– Doesn't one?

The niece laughs. Her hair is the colour of straw and she blushes easily. The old lady herself was dark when young and so was her sister, the girl's mother, but the girl has inherited her father's colouring.

– The question is of no possible interest to me, the old lady says. But Mary keeps asking. Mary's is an insatiable curiosity. Mary would like to know.

– I don't see what concern it is of hers, the girl says.

– It's how she is, the old lady says. She's got an inquisitive nature the way some people have a sweet tooth.

– What do you tell her, Phoebe?

– I tell her I'll ask you.

– And if I don't tell?

– She can reach her own conclusions, the old lady says. I have reached mine and she can reach hers.

The niece laughs and takes her straw hat out from under her chair and fiddles with it.

– She gets more and more restless, the old lady tells her companion later. She can't sit for five minutes without taking that hat out from under her chair and twisting it about in her hands. It drives me mad.

— Why don't you tell her? Mary asks.

— There is such a thing as politeness, the old lady says.
But now she says:

— What good will it do Mary to know? It will only further inflame her mind.

The girl laughs again and lowers her voice, hoping this will cause the old lady to lower hers, for she is very conscious of how thin the walls of the flat are and how easily everything that is said in one room carries to all the others. But the old lady has never lowered her voice in her life and has no intention of doing so now.

— Her curiosity knows no bounds, she says. She is only happy when she is prying and snooping. Even when she knows that I'm not asleep, that I'm merely resting with my eyes closed, and am therefore fully aware of every movement of hers, she cannot resist coming in here and snooping about.

— Oh no, the niece says. I'm sure she doesn't.

— Oh yes she does, the old lady says. She cannot bear to be left out of anything. It's simply more than her nature will bear.

— Perhaps she's only tidying up, the niece says.

— Tidying up my foot, the old lady says.

— Well, someone has to, the niece says.

The old lady lets out a peal of laughter:

— That's what she says. That's exactly what she says when I catch her at it, peering under my bed when she thinks I'm asleep or moving my papers around on the desk. She says someone has to keep things tidy.

— Well, someone does, don't they?

— That sounds horrible, the old lady says.

– What does?

– The way you put that.

– Put what?

– The way you phrased that.

– Oh, the niece says.

– I was never much good at grammar, the old lady says, but my instinct for the language has always been first rate. I wish young people today would speak decent English.

– I'm sorry, the niece says.

– Humpf, the old lady says.

– Anyway, the niece says, she's devoted to you.

– Mary? the old lady says. To me?

– Oh she is, Phoebe! the niece says.

– She is devoted only to herself, the old lady says. But then we all are, aren't we?

– Oh, Phoebe, you don't mean that! the girl says.

– I know what you are implying, the old lady says. But you are an exception, my dear.

– Me? the niece says. I never . . .

And she laughs again in embarrassment.

– There there, the old lady says. Let's change the subject. Tell me about your garden.

– You don't want to hear about my garden.

– No, the old lady says. You're quite right. I don't. Tell me about some of the things that have been happening to you.

Things are always happening to the niece. Her stories show her in such a ridiculous light that they cannot possibly all be true. She has stories about the hospital where she works which are worse than the stories people tell about food canning factories and the kitchens of large restaurants. She also sings in a choir and has stories about that as well.

While she talks the old lady settles back on her pillows and gazes up at the ceiling. It is quite easy to tell when the girl is talking because her voice is both high-pitched and melodious, but it is difficult to catch what exactly it is she is saying. The old lady's voice, on the other hand, carries quite distinctly into all the rooms of the flat.

— Do you think I should get rid of Mary? the old lady asks, suddenly interrupting her.

— Get rid of her?

— I don't think I can stand much more of her, the old lady says.

— Oh, Phoebe, the girl says. Don't be like that.

— I can't stand her snooping, the old lady says.

— She doesn't snoop, the girl says.

— Oh yes she does, the old lady says. I bet you she's out there now, listening at the door to all we're saying.

— How can she be? the girl says. Mike's out there in the hall.

The old lady is silent. Then she says:

— That wouldn't deter her.

— Oh, Phoebe! the girl says.

— She's probably got her door ajar and is listening from her room, the old lady says. Like that she can watch your friend as well.

— Why should she? the girl says. Why should she do a thing like that?

— That's how she is, the old lady says. Snoop, snoop, snoop, that's her.

— You don't mean it, the girl says.

The old lady is silent.

– Don't you think you're imagining it? the girl says.

– I have no imagination, the old lady says.

– Anyway, the girl says with a laugh, who would be interested in what we have to say?

– Mary would, the old lady says. She would want to know if we were saying anything about her.

– Then let's not, the girl says. That would be best, wouldn't it?

– On the contrary, the old lady says. I believe in giving everybody what they want.

– You're just perverse, the girl says.

– Do you think so? the old lady asks, pleased.

– I didn't say that as a compliment, the girl says laughing.

– Oh? the old lady says. Though she is as sharp as a sharp person half her age there are times when things simply pass her by. There is the sense that she watches them do so but cannot rouse up enough interest to pursue them.

She is silent now.

– I was telling you about how I tripped on my dress when we stood up for the final chorus, the girl says.

– Yes yes, the old lady says. She adds: – It's not really very interesting, is it?

– Are you tired? the girl asks.

– I'll tell you when I'm tired, the old lady says. I merely remarked that it wasn't very interesting, which it isn't.

Even the girl is silent after this.

– Do you find it a comfort to have your friend there like that? the old lady finally asks her.

– A comfort?

– I must say I found it made me want to scream

— 20 —

sometimes, the old lady says, when I was married to Robert. The constant proximity of the loved one.

— I'm sure it must be difficult at times, the girl says.

— It's different having Mary here, the old lady says, because our relationship is based on a purely selfish and commercial basis.

— How can you say that, Phoebe? the girl exclaims. You've been friends all your lives.

— That's neither here nor there, the old lady says. It was different then. When we were children and even after she came to work for Father. Now that she is living here with me friendship no longer comes into it. She is dependent on me financially and I am dependent on her physically. Few friendships could survive in such circumstances. Besides, the old lady says, it is better that way. I was friends with Robert, we were even rather intermittently in love, I think, but that made it all the more unbearable to be with him the whole time.

— Oh, Phoebe! the girl says.

— Of course it was different when we had David here, the old lady says. Different for me at any rate. Especially when he was very young.

The old lady is silent, and there is nothing much for the girl to say. In the hall, under the convex mirror, Michael sits scribbling in his notebook. He is always dressed in the same way, in a jacket and tie, but he doesn't look smart, he looks sporty. Partly it is his size and the black hair that keeps falling over his face. At times he looks young, younger even than the girl, and she cannot be as young as she looks. At times he does not look young at all. There are people like that, they change almost completely from day to day.

In the room the old lady says:

— I wonder what is happening to David.

The girl is silent.

— You're sure you haven't heard from him? the old lady asks.

— No, the girl says. Have you?

— I showed you his last letter, didn't I? the old lady says.

— Yes, the girl says.

— From Riyadh, the old lady says.

— Yes, the girl says.

— Let me look at it again, the old lady says. Perhaps he says something about his plans. He was always so full of plans.

The old lady fumbles in her handbag and brings out a faded airmail letter.

— Read it, she says. Tell me what he says.

The girl takes the letter.

— What does he say? the old lady asks, lying back and closing her eyes.

The girl is silent.

— What does he say? the old lady asks again.

The girl is silent.

— Go on, the old lady says.

— He says there's a lot of work being done on the airport, the girl says. That he has a comfortable flat in town. That it is very hot. That there is nothing to do.

— Oh dear, the old lady says. I do hope he's not unhappy.

The girl is staring at the wall of the room across the bed. The letter lies unopened on her lap.

— Do you think he's unhappy? the old lady asks her.

— No, the girl says.

Something in her voice makes the old lady open her eyes and look at her. The girl becomes aware of this and glances down quickly at the letter.

– If only he would marry again, the old lady says, lying back and looking up at the ceiling.

The girl is silent.

– Do you think he will marry again? the old lady asks.

– I don't know, the girl says.

– If only the things that have happened hadn't happened, the old lady says.

– Perhaps it's better that they did, the girl says.

– How can you say that? the old lady says.

– Well, the girl says, who can tell?

– A beautiful wife, the old lady says. A lovely house. And then he had to abandon it all for goodness knows what.

The girl is silent.

– All she wanted to do was break up the marriage, the old lady says.

The girl is silent.

– Otherwise can you explain why they didn't marry? the old lady says. At least that.

The old lady turns her head and looks at the girl.

– Who can tell? the girl says. She puts the letter down on the counterpane.

– You know who she is, don't you, the old lady says suddenly.

– Oh, Phoebe, let's not go into all that again! the girl says.

– You're not trying to shield her, are you? the old lady asks. After all, you're David's friend too, aren't you?

– There there, the girl says.

— No one tells me anything, the old lady says. No one wants to tell me who the girl was and no one wants to tell me if he's all right now. He used to write such beautiful letters when he was a boy.

— He says he's terribly busy, the girl says.

— But before, the old lady says. He never told me this terrible thing about his marriage. It was Mary who found out.

— So you see, the girl says. She has her uses.

— Don't say that! the old lady says sharply.

— I'm sorry, the girl says. I'm sorry, Phoebe.

— Do you want another cup of coffee?

— No, thank you, the girl says.

— Then you'll have some of the other.

— No, thank you, Phoebe, really.

— I will then.

She fumbles in her bag and takes out a key. — Here, she says.

The girl gets up and goes to the corner cupboard. She unlocks it and extracts a bottle. She returns to the bed and fills the empty glass which the old lady holds out to her.

— Is that enough?

— Humpf, the old lady says.

The girl takes the bottle back to the cupboard, locks it in and brings the key back to the old lady.

— Where's my letter? the old lady says, feeling about on the counterpane around her. — Where's David's letter? I must put it away. I can't have it straying. Where is it? Where is it?

The girl finds it and gives it to her. She fumbles with her bag and pushes the letter inside. — I can't start losing things, she says. I can't do that. I must put everything

— 24 —

back where it came from.

Her hands are trembling. She is suddenly agitated.

– It's all right, the girl says. You haven't lost anything. It's all right.

She pats the pillows behind the old lady and pulls the bedclothes straight. The old lady lies there motionless.

– There, the girl says.

– Where's my glass?

The girl hands it to her.

– If I lose things it upsets me for days, the old lady says.

– I'm sure you don't lose much, the girl says.

– I don't, the old lady says. But I have to be careful. Mary will pry.

– Oh, Phoebe! the girl says.

– Oh but she does, the old lady says. There's nothing she wouldn't want to find out.

– But what is there to hide? the girl asks.

– One has one's privacy, the old lady says.

The girl is silent.

The old lady touches her arm. – You know, she says in a loud whisper, it pleases her. About David.

– What about David? the girl says, pretending not to understand.

– It pleased her enormously, the old lady says, smiling and nodding.

– What did?

– That this happened to him, the old lady says.

– Surely not! the girl says.

– It did, the old lady says. It made her feel superior.

– No no, you're imagining it, the girl says.

The old lady laughs. It is more of a bark than a laugh.

– You think you can tell? she says.

– I'm sure you misunderstood, the girl says.

– I could tell by the way she held herself, the old lady says. She held herself triumphantly.

– No no, the girl says feebly.

– Don't say no no like that, the old lady says. I've known her for longer than most people live, after all.

– Don't exaggerate, Phoebe, the girl says.

– It's a fact, the old lady says.

– She told me how upset she was, the girl says.

– Of course! the old lady says. Naturally! She told me that as well. But she wasn't sorry. She wasn't upset. She was jubilant.

– Well, Phoebe, I think you have a jaundiced view of people, the girl says.

– When you're my age, the old lady says, you'll see that everybody *is* yellow. That's just the colour they are.

The girl peals with laughter.

– What have I done with that letter? the old lady says, starting to rummage through her bedclothes. – What have I done with it, damn it?

– You put it in your bag, the girl says.

– No I didn't.

– You did, Phoebe, the girl says. I saw you.

The old lady is hunting through the bedclothes with the glass tilting dangerously in her hand. The girl takes it from her and puts it down on the bedside table.

– I don't know where it's gone, the old lady says.

– May I look in your bag? the girl asks.

– Oh dear, the old lady says. Why does everything disappear like that?

The girl takes the bag and opens it. She looks inside, feels about in the corners, and finally takes out the letter in its airmail envelope, battered by its long residence in the bag and the frequency with which it has been handled.

– Here, she says.

The old lady takes it from her and examines. – Yes, she says. That's it. Where did you find it?

She puts it back in her bag and closes the clasp noisily. She lays the bag on the bed beside her and lies back on the pillows.

– Pass me my glass, she says.

She drinks, holding the glass balanced on her chest.

The girl glances surreptitiously at her watch.

– If you want to go, go, the old lady says. Don't let me detain you.

– Oh no, Phoebe, the girl says. I just . . .

– Have a drink with me then, the old lady says. It's lonely, drinking by oneself.

– No thank you.

– It'll do you good.

– No. Really, Phoebe. Thank you.

– I'll have another then please.

The girl takes the bag, opens it, feels around for the key, finds it, goes to the corner cupboard, unlocks it, takes out the bottle, brings it back to the bed and refills the old lady's glass.

– Don't put it back, the old lady says. We may need it again.

She sips, balancing the glass on her chest. The girl looks down at her hands.

– What do you think is going to happen to him? the old lady asks quietly.

– Happen? the girl says. To whom?

– David of course. Why don't you pay attention?

– I'm sorry, the girl says.

– There's no need to apologize, the old lady says. Just pay attention.

– Yes, Phoebe, the girl says.

The old lady waits. Finally she asks: – Well?

– I think it's terribly good for him to go abroad, the girl says.

– He wouldn't have gone if that woman hadn't broken up the marriage, the old lady says.

The girl is silent.

– And then to go off and leave him high and dry, the old lady says.

– Perhaps it's better this way, the girl says.

– Better? the old lady says. For him to break up his marriage to a beautiful girl and then to be left high and dry like that himself?

The girl says nothing.

– He won't go back to her, the old lady says. He won't tell me why. He just says he won't.

The girl is examining her hands.

– He needs to be looked after, the old lady says. Think what it must be like for him in a foreign city with no one to cook for him and clean his flat.

– Oh I'm sure he has servants for that sort of thing, the girl says.

The old lady is silent. She holds her glass up to the light and peers at it.

– He must have seen through her, she says. He can't have wanted to have anything to do with her once he realized what she was like.

The old lady drains her glass and hands it to the girl,

who puts it on the bedside table.

— Don't you think so? she says.

— Yes, the girl says. I'm sure you're right.

— I wish you'd seen more of him, the old lady says. He was always very fond of you.

The girl says nothing.

— You'd have driven some sense into his head, the old lady says. You'd have warned him away from that girl. He always listened to you. You'd have told him what she was like.

The niece has picked up her straw hat again and is playing with the ribbon.

— He never told you who she was? the old lady asks her.

— No, the girl says.

— Perhaps he'll find somebody nice out there, the old lady says.

— Yes, the girl says.

— He needs domesticity, the old lady says. He's used to being looked after.

— I'm sure he's got lots of servants, the girl says.

— It's not the same thing, the old lady says sharply. Give me another drink.

The girl puts a drop in the bottom of her glass and hands it to her.

— Don't be mean, the old lady says.

The girl says nothing.

The old lady takes the glass. — It's awfully quiet all of a sudden, she says.

The girl settles herself again in her chair.

— I don't like it when it's as quiet as this, the old lady says. It makes me nervous.

The girl says nothing.

– Do you think something's wrong? the old lady asks.

– Wrong, Phoebe?

– When I'm lying here like that, the old lady says, and I can suddenly *hear* the silence – you know? It does funny things to me. I think my heart has stopped. I really think that. It's stopped suddenly and everything is silent.

She mumbles to herself. The girl says nothing.

– She does it on purpose, you know, the old lady says suddenly.

– On purpose? Who?

– Mary. To give me a fright.

– Does what, Phoebe?

– Goes all silent. So that I'll imagine I'm alone in the flat and my heart has stopped.

– Mary? the girl says.

– She does it on purpose.

– How can she? the girl says. You expect her to make a noise all the time?

– She holds her breath, the old lady says. I know she does. To give me a fright.

– You do talk nonsense, Phoebe, the girl says.

– Just listen, the old lady says.

The flat is indeed silent.

– She holds her breath, the old lady says. So that I'll think there's no one there.

– You wouldn't hear her even if she *was* breathing, the girl says.

– I would, the old lady says. I do. I have the sense of another person in the flat.

– But you told me you liked it when she went out. When you had the flat to yourself.

– I do, the old lady says. But then I know she's gone

out. It's when she's here and suddenly she holds her breath that it frightens me. Because then I think it's me that's stopped breathing.

— It could be she who's stopped, the girl says.

— She does it for the legacy, the old lady says.

— What are you talking about? the girl says, lowering her voice instinctively.

The old lady does not lower hers. — She imagines she'll have the flat, she says. When I have passed on. That is what she lives for.

— Oh, Phoebe! the girl says.

— Well, it's natural, the old lady says. She couldn't afford to buy one. Not with the price they are now. It's her only hope.

— You'll outlive us all, the girl says.

— It's these little shocks, the old lady says. These continuous little shocks to the system. That's the way she hopes to hurry me on.

— You mustn't talk like that! the girl says.

— Well, my dear, the old lady says, we must be realistic, mustn't we?

— That's not being realistic, the girl says. That's being mad.

— Well we'll see, the old lady says. We'll see who's mad and who isn't.

There is a silence.

— Your friend must be getting terribly bored, the old lady says.

— No no, the girl says. He wouldn't come if he was bored.

— He could take a stroll along the street, the old lady says. He could have a look at the market.

– He doesn't like that sort of thing, the girl says.

– He just comes to please you? the old lady asks.

– He's never bored, the girl says, and laughs.

– You do see that I couldn't have him in here, don't you? the old lady says.

– I told you, Phoebe, the girl says. He's much happier out there by himself than feeling uncomfortable and unwanted in here. He likes sitting there quietly like that.

– That's what I thought, the old lady says. Besides, we couldn't really talk if he was in here, could we?

The girl is silent.

– If he was in here you might as well not come, the old lady says. We would only be able to exchange banalities instead of really talking as we are doing now.

– He likes sitting out there, the girl says. He's told me so.

– Mary likes it too, the old lady says. She'll have her door ajar and she'll be spying on him.

– Oh I'm sure not, the girl says.

– You know very well that's what she'll be doing, the old lady says.

– I'm sure she has better things to do, the girl says.

– She doesn't have anything to do, the old lady says. That's the trouble. She's bored and so she spies.

– I'm sure she doesn't spy, the girl says.

– Don't be so prim and proper, the old lady says.

The girl is silent.

– She sits in her room with the door ajar and listens to everything that goes on in the flat, the old lady says.

– Well it's not very interesting, is it? the girl says with an embarrassed laugh.

– Even when I'm on my own, the old lady says, I can tell

— 32 —

when she's in her room listening. Sometimes she turns on her telly but I still know she's listening.

— Listening to what? the girl asks.

— Listening to the noises I make, the old lady says. Listening.

— That can't be very exciting, the girl says.

— That shows how little you know about it, the old lady says.

The girl is silent.

— She listens to hear if I get up to pour myself a drink, the old lady says. Sometimes I get up every few minutes to make a hell of a noise with the bottles and glasses just to make her think I'm having another drink. Just to see if she'll find some excuse to barge in and surprise me. What I sometimes do, the old lady says, is to get up very quietly and lock the door as silently as possible, so that she won't know it's locked, and then make a noise with the bottles. Then when she tries to barge in she can't get the door open.

— I'm sure she doesn't listen, the girl says.

— What she does then, the old lady says, is to make a terrific racket banging on the door and shouting so as to fluster me and get me to open the door before I've put the bottles away again. I've been caught once or twice, the old lady confesses. When she bangs like that I do get all flustered and think there's a fire or something. But usually I just tell her to go away.

The girl is silent.

— It's the highlight of her week when you come, the old lady says. Then she has something she can really listen out for.

The girl peals with laughter.

— 33 —

— And now your friend is here it's even better, the old lady says. She puts a hand on her niece's arm and draws her down towards the bed, but she makes no effort to lower her voice. — I wouldn't mind him coming in here you know, she says. I wouldn't mind at all. But if he stays out in the hall it's something for Mary to spy on.

— Oh, Phoebe! the girl says. You're pulling my leg!

— She can watch him through the half-open door, the old lady says. She can see straight down the corridor into the hall.

The girl fidgets in the old lady's grasp.

— And because of the mirror in the hall, the old lady says, she can even see the back of his head.

The girl lets out another peal of embarrassed laughter.

— Of course, the old lady says, it means she can't creep up to the door and listen to us. That's why, she adds, I've been talking more loudly than usual.

— Mary's devoted to you, Phoebe, the girl says.

— Of course she is, the old lady says. I keep her, don't I?

— Well, the girl says, she does a lot for you in turn, doesn't she?

— Perhaps servants *are* better, the old lady says. Then at least you know where you are and you don't have to pretend to be grateful or anything like that.

— And you're really devoted to her, the girl says.

— Of course I am, the old lady says. She's my oldest friend, isn't she? But why should that stop her spying?

— I wish you wouldn't call it spying, the girl says.

— Would you prefer snooping? the old lady asks. I thought spying was a little more dignified.

— People can't help what they hear, the girl says. And, you know, the flat *is* rather small and the walls *are* rather thin.

– They can refrain from kneeling at keyholes and peering, the old lady says.

– I'm sure she's never done that! the girl says.

– She has. She does it all the time.

– Have you ever seen her?

– My dear, the old lady says. How could I? With my leg? I've tried creeping to the door once or twice, taking care to keep out of her line of vision, but I can't help making a noise and of course when I open the door there isn't anyone there.

She motions to the girl to lean over the bed and whispers loudly:

– I've found ash.

– Ash?

– Just outside the door.

– What do you mean ash?

– Cigarette ash.

– Oh, the girl says.

– Well? the old lady says.

– Surely you're not . . .?

– I thought of preserving it, the old lady says. Of putting it in an envelope and challenging her. But then I thought, if it amuses her, let her be. If it amuses her.

– You mean you think she crouches outside your door, smoking and dropping ash on the floor?

– Not on purpose, the old lady says. Of course she doesn't mean to. After all, she doesn't want me to know she's been there. But I was too quick for her.

– But it could have come from anywhere, the girl says.

– Do I smoke? the old lady asks rhetorically.

– Well, it needn't have been cigarette ash, the girl says.

– You don't imagine that after thirty years of living with Robert I don't know cigarette ash when I see it, do you? the old lady asks. Besides, what else could it be?

The niece doesn't answer.

– I've never known such a dirty smoker as Robert, the old lady says. Holes in his pullovers, ash all over the floor, butts in the saucers of his tea and coffee cups and standing straight upright on windowsills and mantel-pieces. He even managed to strew tobacco all over the furniture though he only smoked cigarettes. They would come apart in his hands.

The niece is quite still.

– Just like those cigarettes people make themselves, the old lady says. They would disintegrate. Even the best brands. He only had to touch them.

She lies back on the bed and closes her eyes. She laughs once or twice, deep in her throat, at the memory.

– Do you know, she says, with all his dirty habits there was something so much more *wholesome* about Robert than there is about Mary. Her and her holder. As if anyone smokes with a holder nowadays.

The niece has picked up her straw hat from under her chair and is staring into it.

The old lady opens her eyes but does not move. – Do you know what I mean? she says, staring up at the ceiling.

– Mean?

– When I speak of wholesomeness, the old lady says.

– Yes, the girl says. I . . . think so.

– There was an openness about him which is quite lacking in Mary, the old lady says.

The girl is silent.

– He was so *open*, the old lady says. That is why I feel

— 36 —

he cannot actually have *wanted* to hide anything from me.

— Would you like another drink? the girl asks, half rising.

— Why do *you* think he left like that without a word? the old lady asks, holding out her glass to be refilled.

The girl takes the glass from her, covers the bottom and hands it back to her.

— There must have been a very good reason for it, the old lady says. A reason quite outside his control. Don't you think so?

— I'm sure there was, the girl says.

— He must have wanted to protect me, the old lady says.

The girl sits down again in her chair at the head of the bed.

— Do you know, the old lady says, I sometimes think he must have been a spy.

— Oh, Phoebe! the girl says.

— I have nothing against spies, you know, the old lady says. Real spies. They do a job like anyone else. And at least they are clear about their own motives for what they do. But that would explain why he had to leave like that in a hurry. And was never able to communicate again.

— But spies do communicate, the girl says. Look at Philby.

— Some of them do, the old lady says. The ones who're no use any more except for propaganda purposes. Of course they let those get in touch again. It stands to reason if they're still of use they won't flaunt their presence to the world, doesn't it?

— I . . . suppose so, the girl says.

– If he'd been turned I'd hear from him again, the old lady says. If he'd been turned and escaped. They might invite me to join him, though I don't know if I'd go. But if he's still active they won't let me see him. Not ever again.

The flat is silent except for the murmur from the old lady's bedroom. In the hall, under the mirror, Mike looks up from his notebook and stares into space, sucking his pen. Then he bends over the page again and goes on writing. But the rhythm has been broken. He looks up again, yawns, showing even white teeth, and stretches. He puts the pen and the notebook back in his pockets and gets up.

He walks slowly round the little entrance hall, stopping in turn in front of each of the three framed pictures which hang on the walls, the watercolour landscape painted by Phoebe in her youth, the portrait of her great uncle in his military uniform, and the print of Arundel Castle, and then at the glass cabinet in the corner, with its nine pieces of china dispersed haphazardly about the shelves. He goes down on his haunches and peers at one of the lower shelves, where a small milk-jug with a decoration of little pink chrysanthemums round the border stands rather forlornly by itself. Then he straightens and turns and comes back to the mirror. He takes a comb out of his pocket and sleeks back his hair. As he puts the comb back a lock of hair promptly falls down over his forehead.

He looks round the hall once more, sighs, and sits down again. He crosses his legs and stares at the toe of his polished shoe.

In the room the old lady says:

– You are impatient to be going.

— No no, the girl says.

— Even if you're not, he must be, the old lady says, gesturing in the direction of the door.

— Oh no! the girl says. Oh no!

— Men are impatient creatures, you know, the old lady says. David could never keep still for more than five minutes at a time. Damn. What have I done with that letter?

She feels about on the counterpane around her.

— You put it away, the girl says. It's quite safe.

— I must make sure, the old lady says. She opens her bag and starts to spill its contents out all over the bed.

— It's not here, she says. It's not here. I wonder where it can be.

— Let me see, the girl says.

— I tell you it's not here, the old lady says, a note of panic in her voice.

The girl leans over and spreads the contents of the bag out a little.

— Here it is.

— Where?

— Here.

— Are you sure?

— Isn't this it? the girl says.

— I must be sure, the old lady says. Help me to sit up.

The girl fluffs out the pillows and helps her to sit up higher.

— I must have it, the old lady says. I must find it.

The girl waits, sitting still.

In the hall Mike stands up again, looks round once more, and moves slowly down the room till he is standing at the entrance to the corridor. He walks slowly forward into the darkness. His footsteps make little sound on the thick carpet. He passes one door, which is closed, then one which is slightly ajar, then reaches the door at the end of the corridor, which faces the front door. He opens it and enters, closing it quietly behind him. The bolt is shot home.

In her room the old lady says:

— Thank goodness for that. I wouldn't want to lose it, you know. Though I'm expecting another from him any day now.

The girl starts to put the other items back into the bag. The old lady lies quite still, making no move to help her.

— The prospects out there are excellent, the old lady says. He has a flat with four rooms and a servant.

The girl holds out her hand for the letter and the old lady releases it.

— When he entertains, as he has to, in his position, she says, there is a cook and a butler as well.

The girl is silent.

— It's what's expected of him, the old lady says.

The girl is looking at the wall on the other side of the bed.

— They need to do a lot of building out there, the old lady says. If they're going to play their part in the modern world.

— Engineers are worth their weight in gold out there, she says.

The girl says:

— I'm putting it in here, see. She holds up the letter and the bag.

The old lady nods. — They only want the best of course, she says. The most highly qualified. Those with reputations. They're prepared to pay to get the best.

The girl lays the bag beside her on the counterpane.

— David was never afraid of hard work, the old lady says.

Mike comes out of the bathroom and walks slowly back along the corridor. He appears in the lighted hall and sits down again in the chair by the door. But he makes no move now to take out his notebook and pen.

— I had thought you might make a wife for him, the old lady says. I had hoped, you know, at times.

— Oh, Phoebe, the girl says.

— It would have been nice, the old lady says. He wouldn't have gone off like that if you had married him.

— Of course he would, the girl says. Even quicker.

— No no, the old lady says. It was her. She's a dear girl and so beautiful but she didn't know how to keep him. She couldn't see the danger when it was staring her in the face.

The girl says nothing.

— You've got to know how to keep them, the old lady says. It's common sense. Otherwise everybody gets hurt.

The girl is staring down into the crown of her wide-brimmed hat.

— You've got to have some cunning if you're a woman, the old lady says. It's her fault that David was taken from her. I'm afraid I have to blame her. And then look what happens to him and to me and to everyone. It's no use her feeling sorry for herself afterwards. If it hadn't been for the way she acted none of it would have happened.

The girl is silent, looking into the hat.

— Unless they're spies, of course, the old lady says. Then they're more cunning than you. If they're spies you're at the mercy of their ideology.

She lies back on the pillows and closes her eyes. — What a bore I am today, she says. I haven't asked you anything about yourself.

— Oh but I want to hear about you, the girl says quickly.

The old lady's eyes are open. She is staring up at the ceiling.

— I hope he's done the right thing, she says. Going out to those Eastern places.

The girl is silent.

— He said he would be ever so careful, the old lady says. He assured me he would take every precaution. None of this would have happened if he hadn't been seduced away from his marriage.

— Perhaps he was the seducer, the girl says.

The old lady does not appear to have heard. She says:

— Amanda blamed it on me, you know. She's never come to see me. Not once. Since it happened.

— How could she blame it on you? the girl says.

— She says I never liked her. That I turned him against her.

The old lady looks hard at her niece to see how she is taking this.

— She wrote it all out in a letter, she says.

— What rubbish, the girl says. You were always very fond of her.

— Not as fond as I am of you, the old lady says. You know I always wanted him to marry you.

— Oh, Phoebe! the girl says.

— I did. You would have been eminently suited.

— How can you say that? the girl says. We were always

quarrelling.

– I have never known a quarrel to endanger a marriage, the old lady says. I'm much more worried when couples never quarrel. Besides, she says, you would have given him children.

– Phoebe, the girl says. I don't want to hear you say things like that.

– You would have, the old lady says. Not like her.

The girl is silent.

– Phoebe, she says at last.

– Do you know what she said to me when I blamed her for not having children? the old lady asks.

The girl is looking down at her hands.

– She said it was my fault. With you around how could anyone in their right mind think it would last. That's what she said to me. And how could I be so irresponsible as to have children in that sort of situation. Those are her very words. I didn't deign to reply.

The girl is silent, waiting for the old lady to calm down.

– One just needs to look at you to know you would make a good mother, the old lady says.

– Oh, Phoebe! the girl says.

II

Every morning at seven o'clock sharp, winter or summer, in moonlight or in sunshine, Mary enters Phoebe's bedroom and draws the heavy red velvet curtains.

If she is a minute or two late the old lady rounds on her:

– Did you oversleep? Why are you late?

Mary draws the curtains and ties them back with the yellow cords. – More rain, she says gloomily.

– You're always so gloomy when you feel guilty, aren't you, the old lady says.

– Why guilty?

– It's two minutes past.

– Why should that make me feel guilty?

– You know why, Phoebe says.

Mary gazes down, out of the window, into the gardens.

– Never mind, Phoebe says. Cast off your gloom, Mary. Get me some breakfast. I'm starving.

– Because it's two minutes after you're starving? Mary asks, turning back into the room.

– Don't be a bore, Phoebe says.

Mary sits at her bedside. – I just want to understand, she says.

– The trouble with you, Mary, Phoebe says firmly, is that you can't accept criticism.

– When you accuse me unjustly I have to defend

myself, Mary says. It stands to reason.

On the word 'stands' she stands. Phoebe says:

— There you are. You see what I mean?

— No, I don't, Mary says. I don't suppose I ever shall.

They have breakfast together. Mary has tried having it in the kitchen by herself but Phoebe wouldn't have any of that.

— Am I a leper? she wanted to know. You shun me right through the day but at least you can condescend to have breakfast with me.

— I like to have my breakfast in peace, Mary says.

— Is there a war on here? Phoebe wants to know.

Mary has given up this sort of fight. It is better to submit at the start than later. At least she has the rest of the day more or less to herself.

— It's absolutely pouring now, she says, bringing in the breakfast tray.

— What concern do you think it is of mine what it's like outside? Phoebe says.

— I have to do the shopping, Mary says.

— You should have done it all yesterday.

— Food should be bought fresh every day, Mary says.

— Why do you think I have a fridge? Phoebe asks her.

Mary has laid out her own breakfast things in one corner of the big table which stands against the wall. — It was pouring yesterday as well, she says.

— You chose to settle in this country, Phoebe says. I can't think why you didn't stay in the south of France.

— Geneva, Mary says.

— Geneva. Phoebe says. I can't think why you didn't stay in Geneva.

— The weather's even worse in Geneva, Mary says.

Phoebe is busy buttering her toast.

– Besides, Mary says, you asked me to stay.

– I offered you an arrangement, Phoebe says.

Mary snorts.

– Pigs snort, Phoebe says. Human beings talk.

Phoebe does sometimes get out of bed for lunch, which Mary prepares in the kitchen. She hobbles in, dragging her bad leg, clasping her dressing-gown to her. She is always curious about what Mary has done that morning and what she intends to do in the afternoon.

– I will go to a movie, Mary says.

– Movie? Phoebe says. Movie?

Mary does not rise to the bait.

– Why not say picture-show? Phoebe asks her.

– Why should I say picture-show? Who says picture-show any more?

– Who says movie any more?

– What does one say then?

– Flicks, Phoebe says. Flicks.

– Flicks! Mary says. That went out ages ago.

– No it didn't, Phoebe says.

– Yes it did.

– No it didn't.

Mary busies herself removing the first course, a clear broth out of a tin-foil envelope.

– It didn't, Phoebe says again.

– How do you know? Mary says. You never go out. You don't know how people speak nowadays.

– You don't need to go out, Phoebe says. All you need to do is live in the present.

– Flicks was already old-fashioned in the sixties, Mary says.

– We'll ask Sal, Phoebe says.

– Sal! Mary says.

– Don't say Sal like that, Phoebe says.

– She knows even less about it than you do, Mary says. And that's saying something.

– She is completely at home in the modern world, Phoebe says. Sal is a child of her time.

Mary puts a plate in front of her and heaves the bowl of fruit on to the table.

– How much were those peaches? Phoebe asks.

– Too expensive.

– How much?

Mary takes one, spears it with her fork and starts to peel it with her knife.

– All right all right, Phoebe says. I was only curious.

Mary lays the peel in a little mound at the side of her plate.

– And what are you going to see at the flicks? Phoebe asks, giving way on that one, for it has been agreed between them that the shopping is Mary's domain and she will never be questioned on the subject of prices.

– I may go and see the new Kurosawa, Mary says.

– New? Phoebe says. What do you mean new? Kurosawa died years ago.

– No he didn't, Mary says.

– Of course he did. I remember clearly. Nineteen sixty-nine.

– No he didn't, Mary says, carefully cutting away the last remains of flesh from the peach stone.

– He died in nineteen sixty-nine. In September. We had an Indian summer that year. I remember clearly.

– Kurosawa isn't a day over sixty, Mary says, wiping

the corners of her mouth carefully with the tip of her napkin, then folding it and slipping it into its ring.

— The papers were full of it, Phoebe says. Highest September temperatures recorded this century. India win final test. Death of film genius.

— It must have been another film genius, Mary says.

— Kurosawa, Phoebe says.

Mary takes a drink of water. — His new film, she says. Made last year.

— You must have misunderstood, Phoebe says. It's probably new to the West.

— Kurosawa is not dead, Mary says.

— Yes he is.

— No he isn't.

— Yes he is.

— No he isn't.

— We'll ask Sal.

— Ask who you like, Mary says.

In Phoebe's bedroom, by the bed, is a big velvet bell-pull. Whenever she needs anything Phoebe tugs it sharply. The cord sets a little bell ringing in Mary's room. Sometimes Mary dreams that she is alone in the flat and sleeping in Phoebe's room, in Phoebe's double bed, with the bell-pull within reach. She wakes up for a moment, tugs it, hears it ringing in the other room, empty now, smiles to herself in the dark, and goes back to sleep.

But Mary is not alone in the flat. She is not sleeping in Phoebe's big double bed but in her own single one. It is Phoebe who is sleeping in the double bed, with the bell-pull within easy reach. However, Mary has taken to disconnecting the bell. If Phoebe pulls hard and there is no sound in the rest of the flat she either turns over and thinks of something else to do or gets up and does whatever needed doing herself. When Mary first started disconnecting the bell Phoebe was furious and threatened to throw her out. But Mary pointed out to her that if she did not have some time she could call her own she wouldn't be able to go on living in the flat, and as she evidently meant it Phoebe gave in. At first she tried to impose regular hours on Mary but soon gave up since Mary could disconnect the bell whenever she wanted to.

They have reached an agreement, however, that the bell will never be disconnected at night, because at night it is more likely to be something serious, and because since Mary doesn't sleep too well herself she is often quite pleased to be summoned abruptly and to be able to put on a show of bad temper and then settle down to a long cosy chat. Sometimes she even pretends that the bell has rung though Phoebe insists that she has been fast asleep, that it is Mary coming in in a rush who has woken her, and that she therefore couldn't possibly have pulled the cord.

— You could have pulled it in your sleep, Mary says.
— Don't be ridiculous, Phoebe says.
— That sort of thing can happen.
— Nonsense! Phoebe says.
— Anyway, it rang, Mary says.

Phoebe herself is not averse to a long talk in the middle of the night, even if she has been sleeping soundly until then. Besides, if she dismissed Mary on those occcasions when Mary wanted to talk Mary would probably pretend she hadn't heard anything when it was Phoebe's turn to want to talk.

— What is it now? Mary says, drawing her dressing-gown round her and switching on the main light, for she knows Phoebe particularly dislikes this and she has to do something to get even with her for having woken her up.

— I had a nightmare, Phoebe says. My chest hurts.

Mary stands by the door not saying anything, rubbing the sleep out of her eyes.

— I did, Phoebe says. I woke up terrified. My chest hurts.

— No it doesn't, Mary says.

— It does. I can't breathe properly.

— Of course you can.

— No. I can't

Mary switches off the light and turns to go.

— No! Phoebe calls out. No! Listen! I was frightened. I really was. Mary, she says. Talk to me.

Mary switches on the light again. She stands at the door with one hand on the switch.

— Talk to me, Phoebe says again.

— Does your chest hurt? Mary asks her.

— Yes, Phoebe says. Yes.

Mary switches off the light.

— No! Phoebe calls out. No! It doesn't! It doesn't any more, Mary. It must have been the nightmare that caused it.

Mary waits, a silhouette in the doorway.

— Be a dear and make some tea, Phoebe says.

— You know it will only keep you awake.

— I won't have cocoa, Phoebe says. You know what it does to my insides.

— All right, Mary says. I'll make some camomile tea. It is her favourite beverage.

— I won't have camomile tea, Phoebe says. I want real tea.

Mary crosses the room and switches on the bedside light.

— That's better, Phoebe says.

Mary straightens out the bedclothes. Phoebe sits up and Mary fluffs out the pillows.

— I'll make the tea then, she says.

— Real tea, Phoebe says. Not camomile.

— What was your nightmare about? Mary asks, when she has come back with the tray and sat down at Phoebe's bedside.

— This is absolutely disgusting, Phoebe says, making a face and holding the cup out for Mary to take from her. I told you I wanted real tea.

— It's very good for you, Mary says. It won't keep you awake. She makes no move to take the cup.

— I asked for tea, Phoebe says. Real tea.

— Never mind, Mary says. This'll do you much more good.

— I don't want good done to me, Phoebe says. I want my Ceylon tea.

— What was your nightmare about? Mary asks again as she pours out a cup for herself.

— I don't know, Phoebe says. It was all confused.

— Of course you know, Mary says. Was it about Robert?

— I think it was about my father, Phoebe says.

— Then it was about Robert, Mary says.

Phoebe is silent. Mary looks at her but her eyes are closed.

— What about your father? Mary asks.

— I don't know, Phoebe says. She lies very still in the exact middle of the bed, and keeps her eyes closed.

Mary waits.

— It's all confused, Phoebe says. I saw him dressed in a tiger-skin and carrying a rifle and you know what he thought of big-game hunting.

— I could have fallen in love with your father, Mary says. He was a wonderful man.

— Everybody fell in love with him, Phoebe says.

— I could have too, Mary says.

— But you know what he thought about hunting, Phoebe says. Why should he have appeared to me with a rifle and a huge great tiger-skin with the face hanging down over his shoulder?

— Was it that which frightened you? Mary asks.

— I don't know, Phoebe says.

— Perhaps it was just seeing him, Mary says. I remember dreaming about my own parents and I felt sick when I woke up.

— Don't tell me about your dreams, please, Phoebe says. They are invariably dull.

Mary has no intention of doing so. She half agrees with Phoebe's judgement.

— Was your father alone? she asks.

— He had a puppy in his arms, I think, Phoebe says. And there was something else too. He was holding a letter out for me to read. It was from Robert.

— I told you it was really about Robert, Mary says.

— You know nothing about it, Phoebe says. It was my dream.

— What did he say? Mary asks.

— He was holding it out to me, Phoebe says.

— The puppy?

— No no, Phoebe says. The letter. Why don't you pay

attention?

– I'm paying attention, Mary says. It could have been either.

– How could it have been either? Phoebe says. I explained quite clearly that he was holding the letter out to me to read.

Mary pours herself another cup of tea.

– It contained bad news, Phoebe says. I could tell from his face. He was sitting and comforting me for the bad news.

– I thought you said he was standing, Mary says. With this tiger-skin and this puppy in his arms.

– Do you think I don't know if he was sitting or standing? Phoebe asks.

Mary is pointedly silent.

– Sitting, Phoebe says. And comforting me for the bad news.

– What kind of bad news?

– What kind do you think? Phoebe asks.

– It couldn't have been that he was dead, Mary says. If the letter was from him.

– Perhaps it wasn't from him, Phoebe says. Perhaps it was only about him.

– But you said it was from him.

– I can no longer remember, Phoebe says.

– It may mean you will have news of him soon, Mary says.

– No no, Phoebe says. I will never hear from him again. That is the sacrifice he has had to make.

Mary is clearing away the cups.

– Will you be able to sleep now? she asks.

– No, Phoebe says. Stay with me a little.

– What's the use of my staying?

– Talk to me about Robert. Tell me what you thought of him.

Mary sits again.

– Tell me frankly, Phoebe says. You knew him better than anyone.

– Yes, Mary says. I suppose I did.

– Even me, Phoebe says.

Mary says nothing.

– Married people don't know each other awfully well, Phoebe says. It's as much as they can do to live together. There isn't any energy left over for knowing after that.

– I still don't think he would ever desert you, Mary says.

– What do you mean desert?

– I mean for another woman, Mary says.

– Well, what an idea! Phoebe says.

– It has happened before, Mary says.

– Not to me, Phoebe says. Besides, Robert would never do a thing like that.

– That's just what I'm saying, Mary says. But it's also, she adds, what they all say.

– You are jealous, Phoebe says. That is why you make insinuations of this kind.

– What have I to be jealous about? Mary says.

– You are jealous of our happiness, Phoebe says.

– It does not seem to me that you were very happy, Mary says. If you don't mind my saying so.

– I do, Phoebe says. And you know I do.

– I defend my right to say it, nevertheless, Mary says.

– You can say what you like, Phoebe says. It's a matter of complete indifference to me.

– It was you who brought up the subject, Mary says.

– It wasn't. It was you.

– And who asked me to come and listen to their nightmares? Mary asks.

– Take away this so-called tea, Phoebe says. I have finished with it, and I never want to taste it again.

– And who begged me to stay when I wanted to leave? Mary asks.

– I have finished, Phoebe says. I want to sleep.

– You cannot deny it was you, Mary says.

– Don't be tedious, Phoebe says. Take the things away and let me get some sleep.

– I have a good mind to leave them where they are, Mary says.

– Don't be petty, Phoebe says.

– Besides, she adds, you would only have to clear them away tomorrow morning.

– I have a good mind to leave them here for ever, Mary says. But even as she says this she is putting the cups on the tray.

– Do not wake me in the morning, Phoebe says. I shall be dead to the world.

When Mary had had enough of abroad she wrote to Phoebe: 'Dear Phoebe, I don't suppose you remember me after all this time, but I would very much like to see you. I will be coming back to England for a short time in July and could take the opportunity then.' Phoebe answered promptly: 'I am not a leper. Come to tea at four on the second Friday of the month.'

From the start it was clear that each had a use for the other. Phoebe said:

– How are you living now, Mary?

Mary pretended not to understand and told her where.

— I mean, Phoebe said, what are your prospects?

Mary admitted that they were bleak. But she said she might find some work somewhere.

— At your age? Phoebe said. With your total lack of experience?

— I did work as a secretary once, Mary reminded her.

— You put papers in little piles for Father, Phoebe said. Mary did not contradict her.

— How would you like, Phoebe said, to help me run this flat?

Mary was visibly taken aback.

— Run this flat?

— That's right, Phoebe said.

— Meaning what exactly?

— It's too large for one, Phoebe said.

— Oh, Mary said quickly, I don't think I could afford —

Phoebe cut her short:

— That is not what I was suggesting.

— Then what?

— That you might help me run it. Buy the food and keep the place tidy and so on. And have your own room, in which you could install a television set if you wanted one. And for the rest we could share what space there is. Which, she added, seeing that I'm more or less confined to my bed all the time, means that you'll have the run of the flat.

Though Mary wanted to escape, for many and complex reasons, she also very much wanted to stay.

— I will sack Emily, Phoebe said. I cannot bear to have strangers wandering about my house. Between us we will be able to manage things quite well.

Mary knew this was not the kind of offer you could say you would think about. That would be tantamount to a refusal. And then she would never see Phoebe again. She stood up.

– You can bring your things straight round, Phoebe said. I cannot imagine that you have much luggage.

Though nothing explicit has ever been said, the pattern of their relationship very quickly established itself.

– What I cannot understand, Phoebe says, is why you actually stay. You have more money than I realized at first and could do perfectly well for yourself in some small private hotel in Notting Hill.

Mary lets such remarks pass. When Phoebe takes out her photographs of Robert she sits on the bed and looks them over with her.

– Do you remember him as shy? Phoebe asks her.

– With men you can never tell, Mary says guardedly.

– Marge Symonds told me he had been seen in Amalfi, Phoebe says. With a woman.

Mary waits for the next photo to be passed to her.

– And David said he met someone who had a cousin who had had dinner with him in Rome. Living as man and wife in Rome with an Englishwoman, this man's cousin said.

– You didn't follow it up?

– And risk blowing his cover?

– Blowing his – ?

– I always had complete faith in him, Phoebe says. Of course he was an idealist. But so many men are.

– There was something about him, though, Mary says. Something depressive.

– Robert was never depressive, Phoebe says. If anything, you are the gloomy one.

— I never said anything about gloom, Mary says. I said depressive. They are not at all the same thing.

— Your theories always incline towards the eccentric, Phoebe says.

— His idealism and his loyalty, Phoebe says. I am talking, she adds, about his loyalty to me.

— He always smelled a bit of scent, Mary says. I found that slightly disconcerting.

— I would hardly have thought something like that would disturb you, Phoebe says. When you put that pine essence in your bath you pour so much in I have to get up and open the windows in here, though there are two closed doors and the length of the corridor between us.

In the early days of their companionship Phoebe would talk at length about her son David. Now that she can do so on Saturdays to her niece she has less to say to Mary on this topic. But she still occasionally brings it up.

— They were an ideal couple, she says. Ideally suited.

Mary knows better than to interrupt.

— Do you think it's my fault he's so weak? Phoebe asks her. That he lets himself be swayed so easily?

— Who can tell? Mary says. Early upbringing accounts for so much in later life.

— Of course, Phoebe goes on, you wouldn't know about that sort of thing.

— What sort of thing?

— Children, Phoebe says.

Mary shrugs.

— I don't blame him, though, Phoebe says. He would never have done what he did without provocation. I'm sure of that. It was the woman led him on. Whoever she was.

Mary is silent.

— It's a relief he got rid of her, anyway, Phoebe says.

— Who can tell with love? Mary says.

— That is a crass remark, Phoebe says.

Mary is unwilling to make a fight of it.

— Is that where love leads you? Phoebe asks her. To a four-room flat with air-conditioning and two different kinds of shower in the middle of the desert? When you have a perfectly good wife and home waiting for you in Twickenham?

— Would she have him back? Mary asks.

— Of course she would, Phoebe says. It's only his pride that won't let him come back.

— If only they'd had children, Mary says.

— They were far too intelligent to rush into that sort of thing the moment the register was signed, Phoebe says.

— I only meant it would have been more of a hold on him, Mary says.

— That only shows how little you know about it, Phoebe says. It would simply have meant double the heartache. Now go away and leave me alone. I need to think.

But Phoebe is as likely to want company as she is to want to be alone. When Mary has been out to the cinema or even just shopping Phoebe will peremptorily tug at her bell-pull if she does not come straight in to report. And the moment Mary is inside the bedroom she asks her sharply why she has been out so long.

— It was a long film, Mary says.

— You're sure you didn't go to sleep and find yourself still there in the middle of the next showing? Phoebe asks her.

Mary does not deign to reply to such an accusation.

— It would be perfectly natural, Phoebe says. I kept you up most of the night, forcing you to listen to my nightmares.

— I was happy to listen, Mary says.

— I know you were, Phoebe says. They were a good deal more interesting I'm sure than the inside of Mr Alfredo Kurosawa's head.

— Akiro, Mary says, but Phoebe is convinced that the distinguished film-maker's mother was Spanish and that he is or rather was called Alfredo.

— You're not going to correct me about that at my age, she says, whenever the topic comes up, which is oftener than might be expected.

— Age has nothing to do with it, Mary says. Everyone knows he's called Akiro.

— I'm sorry, Phoebe says. Everybody knows he's called Alfredo.

— Akiro, Mary says, for she cannot all the same let it pass.

— His mother was Spanish, you see, Phoebe explains.

— I've never heard that, Mary says.

— There's a lot you haven't heard, Phoebe says.

— I would know if she had been, Mary says.

— It's clear that you wouldn't, Phoebe says, since you don't.

— I brought you a book, Mary says. I showed you. *The Films of Akiro Kurosawa*.

— What do I care about books? Phoebe says. Everyone knows he's called Alfredo. It's common knowledge.

Mary is silent, pursing her lips.

— I don't remember a book, Phoebe says. What sort of cover did it have?

— It had the famous scene from *Throne of Blood*, Mary says.

— I never knew that *Throne of Blood* had only one famous scene, Phoebe said. I asked you what the cover represented.

— Well, Mary says, in the top right-hand corner —

— I don't remember any books, Phoebe says, interrupting her. Besides, books are nearly always wrong.

— Not about things like that, Mary says.

— About everything, Phoebe says. As soon as you know the least thing about any subject you find that books on that subject are riddled with errors.

— We'll ask Sal, Mary says.

— You can ask her if you like, Phoebe says. But I doubt if she knows anything about the subject at all.

— Everyone knows he's called Akiro, Mary says.

Phoebe has decided to bring this particular part of the conversation to an end: — Sal is a dear girl, she says, but I sometimes wonder if she's entirely sane.

— Is anyone entirely sane? Mary asks.

— Nonsense! Phoebe says. Wishy-washy nonsense!

Mary sits on the bed picking through the photos Phoebe has been looking at in her absence.

— I don't remember that one of all three of us, she says. Do you remember who took it?

— Of course I do, Phoebe says. It was Freddy. I've rarely known anyone less efficient with a camera than he was.

— It seems quite good to me, Mary says.

— If I may say so Mary, Phoebe says, you don't know

the first thing about photography.

— It's not a work of art, if that's what you mean, Mary says.

— That's not what I mean, Phoebe says. I mean that the house looks as though it's falling down and half my right arm is missing.

— He's caught the expressions, Mary says.

— If you mean that I'm the only one who seems to be aware of the fact that the house is falling down, Phoebe says, then I have to agree with you.

Sometimes Mary sits in the armchair by the window and knits while Phoebe plays patience on the counterpane. Occasionally she nods off and it seems to her that she is somewhere quite different, by the sea, in a far-off land, or at the very least in her own bed in her own room.

Phoebe sometimes looks up from her game and tries to catch Mary's eye. Mary's face remains expressionless, her lips moving as she counts the stitches or whispers to herself.

— I wish you wouldn't wear the same expression all the time, Phoebe says. As if you were afraid to show any emotion.

Mary smiles a little at that, still counting under her breath, then her face resumes its habitual expression.

— You must have been very frightened as a child, Phoebe says. You must have forced yourself to hide any emotion you felt. That would explain it.

Mary does not contradict her.

— Robert often commented on your sullen expression, Phoebe says. He felt you were afraid to let yourself go. When she does finally let go, he used to say, watch out.

Mary goes on with her knitting.

– But you never did, Phoebe says. Did you?

Mary does not look up.

– Did you? Phoebe asks her again.

Mary stands at the door of Phoebe's room, her shopping bag in her hand.

– Of course it's a form of self-defence, Phoebe says. But the trouble is that after a while it starts to stifle your inner life. You must make an effort, Mary, or you'll freeze inside in conformity with your frozen exterior. You must make a real effort to laugh more.

– I laughed a lot today, Mary says.

Phoebe is too busy putting away her cards to reply to this.

– There was someone at the butcher's with a very big dog and a very small dog, Mary says. I really laughed.

– A very big dog and a very small dog, Phoebe says. You really laughed.

– Well, everyone was laughing. Mary says defensively. I wasn't the only one.

– A big dog and a small dog, Phoebe says. What's so funny about that?

– Everybody was laughing, Mary says.

Phoebe looks at her, waiting for her to go on, but she just stands in the doorway, looking in, the shopping bag dangling from her arm.

– Why? Phoebe says.

– I don't know, Mary says. I don't know, she says again.

– You probably want to put those things away in the fridge, Phoebe says.

But Mary stands there, not moving. – Not quite everybody, she says. The woman at the till didn't laugh.

But everybody else did.

– Oh yes? Phoebe says.

– I was one of those who laughed, Mary says. I don't know why.

– Well don't ask me, Phoebe says.

Mary looks down at her bag. – They always laugh a lot in there, she says. I don't know why.

Phoebe closes her eyes. She appears to be asleep.

Mary turns. She moves slowly off towards the kitchen.

– Mary! Phoebe calls after her.

Mary comes back. She stands in the doorway.

– The door, Phoebe says. Shut the door.

Mary shuts the door. Phoebe hears her dragging her feet down the corridor on her way to the kitchen.

III

The old lady has a way of screwing up her face and almost closing her eyes when she wants to look particularly closely at the person she is talking to. – Are you going to marry him? she asks.

The niece laughs.

– Are you? the old lady presses.

– I don't know.

– You should, the old lady says. Time isn't standing still.

– Actually I'm not sure that I should, the niece says.

– In general do you mean? Or him in particular?

– Both, the niece says.

– I often think you should have married David, the old lady says.

– Oh, Phoebe! the niece says.

The girl looks down into the crown of her big straw hat.

– I wish he'd told me he was involved with another woman, the old lady says. Who knows, I might have been able to help him.

The niece is examining the rim of her hat.

– He never told you? the old lady asks.

– Told me what?

– That he was leaving his wife and home, the old lady says.

The sunlight is falling right across the old lady's face.

– Do you want me to draw the curtains a little, Phoebe? the girl asks.

– Yes, do that dear, the old lady says.

When the girl has sat down again at the head of the bed the old lady says:

– I had a feeling he might have told you.

– Me? the girl says. Why me?

– I don't know, the old lady says, looking at her. It was just a hunch.

Outside, in the hall, Mike looks up from his notebook and stares down the dark corridor. He does not move for a minute or two, then, as if coming to a sudden decision, bends again over his notebook, biting his lower lip. The pen flies over the white page.

– I lie here, the old lady says, and I can't help thinking. I think about all sorts of things.

– What things? the niece asks.

– He phoned me, you know, the old lady says. The day he left. I think he was about to tell me but he didn't.

– Tell you?

– Yes. Who she was.

– But he didn't?

– I think he was about to, the old lady says.

– What do you mean you think he was about to? the girl asks.

But the old lady no longer seems to be paying attention. She has closed her eyes and is lying back in bed. She says, without opening her eyes:

– I found a photograph. The other day. I mean I looked

at it closely. It was a photograph I had often looked at. Of Robert and me when we were first married. With Mary.

She is silent. The girl waits.

– Here, the old lady says, struggling to sit up. Let me show you.

She hunts about in her bag and produces a photo. She holds it out to the girl, who puts her hat down on the floor under her chair and takes it from her.

– Well? the old lady says, looking at her.

The girl holds the photo a little way from her and examines it.

– Well? the old lady says again.

– I don't . . .

– Don't you notice anything?

– No, I . . . I've seen it before, the girl says, handing it back.

– No, no, the old lady says, waving it away. Look again. Do you see anything odd about it?

The girl looks.

– Well? the old lady says again.

– You mean the hats?

– Hats be damned, the old lady says. Something odd, I said.

– All I can see that looks odd are the hats, the girl says. And the house seems to be tilting a little.

– That's just Freddy, the old lady says. He couldn't hold a camera steady for a second.

The girl puts the photo down on the counterpane beside the old lady.

– Just look, the old lady says, holding it out to her again. Look hard.

The girl holds the picture in front of her. She turns it

this way and that in the light. Finally she says:

— No. I'm sorry, Phoebe.

— Look along the middle of the picture. Along the middle.

— I'm sorry, Phoebe, I —

— Look at the hands.

The girl brings the photo up close. — The hands? she says.

— Don't you see anything?

— Like what?

— Look. Just look.

— I'm sorry, Phoebe, I really, I —

— Doesn't it seem to you, the old lady says, that Robert and Mary are holding hands?

— Holding ha — ?

— What do you think? the old lady asks, smiling up at her.

The girl has the photo up close to her face.

— Well? the old lady says.

— One can't really see the hands at all, the girl says.

— I admit I didn't take it in at first, the old lady says. I was too busy trying to reconstitute my missing right arm. But the more one looks the clearer it gets.

— I don't really see anything, the girl says.

The old lady takes the photo from her and holds it up in proof.

— Mary might remember, though, the girl says.

The old lady is now busy in her turn examining the photo.

— Have you asked her? the girl says.

The old lady looks at her over the photo.

— Have you? the girl asks again.

– Would you? the old lady says. If you were in my place?

– Well, surely, it's rather amusing, if . . .

– I don't think, the old lady says, that if you were to reflect on the matter you would suggest, as you are doing, that it was rather amusing.

– What do you mean, Phoebe?

– What do you think I mean?

The girl picks up her hat again and starts to examine it.

– What do you know about Robert? the old lady asks her.

– Well, you told me . . .

– What? What did I tell you?

– Well . . . spies . . . and . . .

The old lady is watching her intently.

– I don't know. I . . .

The old lady hasn't moved.

– Oh, Phoebe! the girl says.

The old lady shakes her head.

– But you . . .?

– Spies! the old lady says. What a lot of nonsense! People have spies on the brain these days.

– Then what . . .?

– What do you think?

– I don't know, the girl says quickly. She gets up. – I must go, Phoebe, she says. I really must go.

– Not before I've finished telling you what I think.

The girl says in a whisper:

– No, Phoebe, please! You mustn't torment yourself like that. You really mustn't.

– Living in Rome with a woman posing as his wife, Phoebe says. Sighted with an Englishwoman in Amalfi.

– But . . .?

– My best friend, the old lady says. Living in so-called Geneva. Doesn't it make you think?

– Oh, Phoebe! the girl says.

– Well, doesn't it?

– But then why did she . . .? I mean . . .?

– If he tired of me he'd tire of her, wouldn't he? the old lady says. It stands to reason. Amalfi or no Amalfi.

– And yet you . . .?

– I what?

– Never mind.

– I what?

– But why then should she . . .?

– What? Write? Come here? Decide to stay?

The girl looks at her unhappily.

– Well, we're old friends, aren't we? the old lady says. We were friends before either of us knew him. Besides, she's curious to see if I will ever realize. And I'm curious to see if she will ever realize that I have realized. Or perhaps she wants to atone. Wants me to forgive her. But you see, the old lady says, I will only forgive her if she confesses openly, and she will only confess if she is certain that I will forgive her. Isn't that an interesting situation?

– You mustn't talk like that, the niece says. It's not right. I won't have you torment yourself like that, Phoebe.

– It's not a torment, the old lady says. It's something that's both curious and interesting. It gives us something to do, after all.

– Oh, Phoebe! the girl says.

– Mary has her listening sessions when you're in here with me, the old lady says. And I too in my way listen and

— 72 —

watch. She listens to me and I listen to her. She watches me and I watch her.

— Oh dear, the girl says. I don't know why you get ideas like that, Phoebe. The hands are really quite blurred on the photograph. Quite blurred. There's nothing to go on at all. I don't know why you ever thought up things like that.

— Let's say I just grew tired of spies, the old lady says, looking straight at her and not blinking.

The girl blushes. — I must go, she says. She bends and kisses the old lady hurriedly on both cheeks and then, holding her straw hat firmly in her hand, runs towards the door.

IV

— It was only because I was bored, the old lady says to her companion.

— Only because you were bored?

— Well, the old lady says, that was one of the reasons. There were others, of course. There always are.

— And you told her that? Mary says.

— I thought it would be interesting to see how she reacted.

Mary looks at the photograph.

— Give it to me, the old lady says. She takes it from her and puts it away in her handbag. — You weren't holding his hand, were you? she asks.

Mary is busy drawing back the curtains to let in the afternoon sun.

— It was when we were looking at it the other day, the old lady says. It was then I thought I would make that suggestion.

Mary fastens back the curtains and turns towards the bed again.

— I also told her you were the one, the old lady says. I told her you were the one sighted with him in Amalfi.

— Me? Mary says.

— I don't know if she believed me.

— Me? Mary says again. In Amalfi? With him?

– That's what I suggested, the old lady says. I was interested in her reaction.

– But . . .?

– I tried to make it as convincing as possible, the old lady says. I suggested that after a few years he tired of you, as he had tired of me. That then you came back here and naturally wanted to see if I suspected anything. Or perhaps in some obscure way to atone for what you had done.

– What a nonsense, Mary says.

– Yes, Phoebe says. Perhaps it was. But I had my reasons.

Mary pulls the bedclothes straight as best she can with Phoebe inside the bed and making no move to help her. She says:

– What reasons?

– I wondered when you'd ask that, Phoebe says.

– Oh?

– Yes, Phoebe says.

– She lies back in the bed and closes her eyes.

– What reasons then? Mary asks her.

– Well, you see, Phoebe says, it suddenly came to me. When I was talking to her about David.

She is silent. Mary waits a while. Then, when it is clear that the other will not speak again of her own accord, she says:

– It came to you?

– That's right.

– What did?

– You don't see?

– See what?

– What I'm driving at?

Mary shakes her head.

— A sort of insight, Phoebe says. A sort of vision. Of her and David.

— Her and David?

— I had a vision of what had happened.

— Happened? To whom?

— Well, to them of course, Phoebe says.

— To them?

— I wish you wouldn't keep repeating my words, Phoebe says.

— I'm sorry, Mary says. But she stands there, waiting.

— I realized that she was the one, Phoebe says. It suddenly came to me. That she'd been the one all the time.

— She? Mary says uncertainly.

— Yes, Phoebe says. She. Who broke up the marriage.

— What marriage?

— Aren't you feeling well? the old lady asks her.

— Of course I'm feeling well. Why?

— You don't seem to be able to concentrate very well.

— I'm perfectly well, Mary says. It's you who're incoherent.

Phoebe sighs. — What marriage? she says. David's, of course. What do you think I'm talking about?

— David's? Mary says.

— I wish you'd stop repeating everything after me, Phoebe says. What is the matter with you today?

Mary is silent, peeved.

— It was so obvious, Phoebe says. I wondered why I'd never thought of it before.

— David's? Mary says. Sal?

— And the irony is, Phoebe says, that I wanted them to

marry all along. But David had set his heart on Amanda. And then, of course, he tired of her, as I knew he would.

— And then, you think . . . ?

— Well, don't you?

— What nonsense! Mary says, pressing her lips together.

— You're so innocent, Phoebe says. You're so innocent, Mary.

— But why should she — ?

— Come here? All the time? Is that what you mean? But that's what gave me the idea for the other thing. About you and Robert. I think she comes partly out of curiosity, to see if I suspect, and partly out of guilt, to expiate.

— Ex — ?

Phoebe is silent. Mary says:

— I think it's a lot of nonsense.

— I expect they had been having an affair for some time, Phoebe says. And when Amanda found out she made a terrible fuss. And, as often happens in such cases, it wrecked not just the marriage but the affair as well. That's when David decided to go abroad.

Mary is silent.

— Didn't it surprise you that Sal should suddenly turn up again after all these years?

— It wasn't suddenly. She . . .

— She what?

— Well, Mary says, she used to come and see you before. And then she was in Edinburgh. So she . . .

— Once a year, Phoebe says. Once a year she came to visit me before. And how often is it now? Once a week. Every week. Summer or winter. Rain or shine.

— Well, she said she —

— She said she what?

— Well, Mary says, that things had not been easy for her. That there had been complicating factors. That her private life . . .

— Well? Phoebe says. Well?

— You can't really believe that, Mary says.

— Why not?

— It's not . . . natural.

— Natural? Phoebe says. Who said anything about nature?

— What about evidence? Mary says. You don't have any evidence. Not for any of this.

— Oh, evidence! the old lady says. Who cares about evidence? Doesn't it all fit together? Doesn't it?

— Did you ask her?

— Me? the old lady says. I told you what I did. She stares at her companion.

— I'll make some tea, Mary says.

— She wouldn't look at me, the old lady says. She wouldn't look at me when I talked to her about David. It was then that I understood. And you know, the old lady says, the other day, when I wove that fanciful story about you and Robert, I tried to look into her eyes but she kept turning away. And then I knew that she knew I knew.

— What rubbish, Mary says. You know nothing. Do you understand? Nothing at all.

Phoebe is looking at her. Mary stalks to the door, stops, looks round. The old lady is still looking straight at her.

— Really! Mary says.

The old lady smiles, then lies back in bed and starts to laugh.

— Why do you laugh? Mary asks her. Why do you laugh like that?

The old lady stops laughing abruptly. She says up into the air of the room:

— You know why I laugh. You know only too well why I laugh. Only too well. Only too well.

V

Some days, when the niece visits, the old lady is in a melancholy mood. – It won't last much longer, she says. Thank God for that.

– You mustn't speak like that, Phoebe! the niece says.

– I can feel it coming, the old lady says. I can feel it in my bones. Thank goodness for that.

The niece spins the straw hat nervously in her hands. – She didn't stop the whole time she was here, the old lady tells her companion afterwards. It nearly drove me mad.

– You could say something to her about it, the companion suggests.

– When she's come all the way from Highgate and given up her Saturday for me? the old lady says.

Now she says:

– It's gone on long enough. Only the dregs are left. I'll be glad when it's over.

– Have you been quarrelling with Mary again? the niece asks.

– You know we don't quarrel, the old lady says. All I hope is that I don't suffer too much and don't lose all my wits. I would hate to lose all my wits.

– You'll see us into the grave, the niece says.

– And what good would that do me? the old lady asks. I'll still have to come to it myself in the end.

There is a silence in the room.

The old lady says:

— If only it were the other way round. If only one died right at the start and got that over with instead of having to wait for it all one's life. That's what I can't stand. The waiting for it all one's life. And then not to be able to talk about it afterwards.

She is silent. Then she says:

— If it was the other way round there would be birth to look forward to, wouldn't there?

— That's what Christianity says, the girl says.

— Christianity my foot, the old lady says.

The girl is silent again.

— There was something I was going ask you, the old lady says. But now it's left me.

— What kind of thing, Phoebe?

— Something I was saving up to ask you. But now I can't remember.

— Do you want me to ask Mary?

— What on earth for?

— I thought perhaps it was to do with an argument you might have had.

— We never argue, the old lady says.

The girl waits.

— Something you said just now put me in mind of it, the old lady says. But now I've forgotten again.

— Was it to do with religion? the girl asks.

— No, no, the old lady says. Why should it have anything to do with religion?

The girl is silent.

— I remember now, the old lady says.

The girl waits. When the old lady remains silent she

says:

— Yes?

— I've remembered, the old lady says. But it wasn't that. It was something else. Now tell me about your work.

— Oh, Phoebe, the girl says.

— What's the matter with you?

— I don't want to talk about that, the girl says.

— Well, we have to talk about something, the old lady says.

— I could leave, the girl says. If you're not in the mood to talk today.

— No, don't do that, the old lady says quickly. I like to have you here even if we don't talk at all. You know that.

Outside, in the little hall, Mike looks up from his notebook and stares down the dark corridor. Though the walls in the flat are thin, the flat itself is well insulated from the rest of the building and from the world outside. No sound reaches the hall except for the murmur of conversation in the old lady's room.

— I think, the old lady says, that I have found out the identity of the other woman. I am on her track.

— Oh, Phoebe, the girl says.

— I mean the woman who broke up David's marriage, the old lady says.

— On her track? the girl says. How do you mean?

— I have a clue, the old lady says. I am in the process of investigating.

— I wish you wouldn't worry about that any more, the girl says. After all, it's over and done with, isn't it?

— I have my curiosity to satisfy, the old lady says. I don't like loose threads.

The girl is silent. Then, when the old lady shows no

sign of speaking, she says:

— He's written to you again?

— He has, the old lady says. I'm sure he has. Innumerable times. But you know what happens to letters out there. If they aren't censored they get lost. Either they arrive a year after they're written or they don't arrive at all. And of course he knows I hate the phone.

Sometimes, after a morning with the old lady, the girl slips into Mary's room, sits on the desk, dangling her legs, and has a brief chat with her. She is a great one for bringing books one week and then expecting people to have read them and formed an opinion by the next.

— Have you read this? she says. *The Life of the Cat. The White Tower. The Medieval Garden.*

Mary reads all the flower and animal books, though she doesn't like animals. She has told the girl often enough that she can't read history, that the facts slip out of her mind as soon as they enter, but the girl keeps forgetting. — This one's good, she says. *The Last Days of Paris. Bury My Heart at Wounded Knee. Alexander the Great. Mohamed: The Prophet's Life.*

In the little hall, under the convex mirror, Mike looks up from his notebook. He examines the toe of his polished shoe. Then he uncrosses his legs and stands up.

He walks once round the little hall, examining in turn each of three pictures, the watercolour, the family portrait, and the print. He stops at the glass cabinet in the corner and sits on his haunches, looking intently at the rather dusty objects dispersed about the shelves.

In the room the old lady says:

— I have decided to leave the flat to you. I have made my will accordingly.

– I don't want to hear, the girl says.

– You must hear, the old lady says. I am telling you so that you will know.

– I don't want to know, the girl says.

– That is irrational, my dear, the old lady says.

– I just don't want to know, the girl says. Can't you understand that, Phoebe?

– No, I can't, the old lady says. Why can't you take things as they are? Why do you have to pretend that they don't exist?

– Oh, Phoebe, the girl says. Let's change the subject, please.

– Of course I might change my mind again, the old lady says. If I was sure Mary would outlive me of course I would leave it to her.

The girl gets up.

– You're not going already? Phoebe says.

– Yes. I have to.

– But you've only just come!

– Oh, Phoebe! the girl says.

– I'm such a boring old thing, Phoebe says.

– I told you, the girl says. I told you we had to leave early today.

– Is your friend playing rugby again? the old lady asks.

– No. He has to bring the car round to be seen to.

– On a Saturday? the old lady says.

– And I want to look in on poor Mary before we go.

– Poor Mary! the old lady says. Why poor Mary?

– Oh, Phoebe! the girl says.

– What do you want to look in on her for?

– I have some books for her.

– In that bag?

– Yes.

– She never reads them, the old lady says. She only pretends to to please you.

– She reads some of them, the girl says.

– I don't think she reads any.

The girl is standing by the door. – Goodbye, Phoebe, she says.

– It's wasted on her, the old lady says. She hasn't an ounce of brains in her head.

The girl is standing at the door.

– Phoebe, she says.

The old lady opens her eyes and turns her head slightly so as to look at her.

– Goodbye, the girl says.

The old lady does not move. Her eyes rest on the girl's face, unblinkingly.

The girl opens the door.

VI

Robert wakes up in the bedroom of his flat in Positano. It seems to him that his wife is in the room and speaking to him. He has not heard her voice or thought of her in years. But now, as he drifts off to sleep again, he imagines the life she is leading, in her flat in the heart of London, with the companion of her old age. In his half-sleep he hears their conversation as clearly as if they had been in the room with him. Yet, curiously, he cannot understand anything they are saying.

He cannot sleep any more. He gets up and goes to the window. The sea is there, beneath him, as still and blue as ever. He goes to the wardrobe and opens it. He looks through the clothes with which it is filled. Sally did not take any of them with her when she left. Perhaps this means that she intends to return. He does not think so. He tries to imagine what she is up to, but since she will not answer any of his letters he does not succeed.

He finds that he is not standing in front of the open wardrobe but is still in bed. Perhaps he should get rid of the clothes? Give them away? Send them back? As he does every day, he defers a decision. He decides instead to have breakfast on the balcony.

He shaves. He dresses. He lays out the breakfast things. Yes, he thinks, another day has begun. But his mind is elsewhere.

VII

Sometimes Mary lies in the large bed which once belonged to Phoebe and which, like the flat and the rest of its contents, has passed to her. She closes her eyes and tries to imagine what it must have been like to be Phoebe, to have been Phoebe. She tries to remember the two of them at school and then later, at different moments of their lives, together and apart. But it never works. She can only think about it, if she manages to think about it at all, as she would about the lives of two people she has known only moderately well, two people wholly unconnected with herself.

Most of the time she sits in her room, at her desk, with the door ajar, listening to the noises in the flat. Or she closes the door and lies on her bed and stares up at the ceiling. Or sits in the armchair and does the crossword puzzle in the previous day's paper. Occasionally she watches TV, as she always did, on the small portable she bought herself when she moved in with Phoebe. But the images, now as then, fail to catch her interest, and she often finds herself thinking about something else while the meaningless images go on flickering on the small screen in front of her.

She gets up and roams through the flat. Her feet, in their slippers as usual, make no noise on the carpets. She haunts the flat like a ghost, gliding down the corridor and into the entrance hall where the man once sat, week after week, waiting for the girl to finish with the old lady, and on into Phoebe's bedroom, till she stands at the window, looking down into the garden below as with one hand she holds up the curtain.

She sits silent at her desk, watching, waiting, as she did when Phoebe was alive. Even when there was no one in the flat except for Phoebe she would sit as she sits now, at her desk with the door open or ajar, listening to the sounds wafting from the other's room.

If she hears Phoebe get out of bed, which she occasionally does by herself, Mary's instinct is to close the door quickly or, if there isn't time, to leave her place at the desk and lie down on the bed and close her eyes. But Phoebe does not look in, on her way to the bathroom or the kitchen. She could be alone in the flat for all the awareness she seems to show of her friend's presence. Yet when Mary has been out to the cinema or shopping Phoebe will peremptorily ring the bell as soon as she is inside the front door and not stop until Mary has opened the door of her room. Then she asks her sharply why she has been out so long.

— It was a long film, Mary says.

— You're sure you didn't go to sleep and find yourself still there in the middle of the next showing? Phoebe asks her.

Mary does not deign to reply to such accusations.

— It would be perfectly natural, Phoebe says. I kept you up most of last night, forcing you to listen to my dreams.

— I was happy to listen, Mary says.

— I know you were, Phoebe says. At least they were a

good deal more interesting than the lucubrations of Mr Alfredo Kurosawa.

– Akiro.

– Alfredo.

– Akiro Kurosawa.

– You're not going to correct me about that at my age, are you? Phoebe says.

– What has age to do with it?

– Age has a great deal to do with it, Phoebe says.

Now Mary sits at her desk, her elbows on the leather top, her chin in her hands. The even morning light bathes the room. All the windows in the flat are shut, as they have always been, effectively sealing it off from the world outside.

In the master bedroom Phoebe is saying to her niece:

– Sometimes I think it would be better if I had a servant or a maid. Then at least I would know where I was and she would know where she was.

The niece laughs her spontaneous gurgle, which hides embarrassment and simultaneously expresses high spirits.

– I suspect, though, the old lady says, that I also take some satisfaction from doing what I can for a friend who has always been so much less fortunate than me.

She adds, with her usual honesty:

– And some satisfaction from the chance our little arrangement gives me to boss someone about without quite having the right.

– Oh, Phoebe! the niece says.

The man sits in the hall, his legs crossed, staring at the toe of his ridiculous shoe. All his clothes look comfortable and expensive. He always wears a jacket and tie.

Sometimes he takes a notebook from one of the pockets of his jacket and a pen from another and places the notebook precariously on the arm of the chair and writes, without looking up, his face tense with the effort of concentration.

When he is thus absorbed he seems to notice nothing around him, not even the occasional bump or thud in one of the rooms whose doors are closed or almost closed, or in the corridor which runs down the length of the flat from the little entrance hall where he sits to the kitchen.

In the master bedroom, raising her voice so that what she says will carry through the thin walls of the flat, Phoebe says to her niece:

— It came to me quite suddenly, but with perfect clarity. It could only have been Mary.

— Oh, Phoebe! the niece exclaims.

— That he was always so critical of her should have aroused my suspicions earlier. Phoebe says. My best friend and my husband. To think of it happening to me.

— But why should she come back here then? the niece asks. Surely you're the last person she'd want to see if what you say is true?

— She was my best friend, Phoebe says.

— Yes but if – ?

— I am still her best friend, Phoebe says. You are too innocent. You don't understand how people's minds work.

— But – ?

— I am the only person left here, Phoebe says. For her. And besides, she feels guilty. She wants me to forgive her. Also she feels curious. She wants to see if I will ever understand. Every day she thinks she is going to tell me.

She would like to tell me. She feels the need to tell me. But every day prudence prevails. Prudence prevails. But at the same time the desire to tell me mounts. The desire to see my face when she tells me. And still prudence prevails.

– Oh, Phoebe! the niece says.

Sometimes Mary goes to sleep in the big bed in which Phoebe spent her days and in which she eventually died. She goes to sleep there and when she wakes up it is night and the curtains are not drawn, which gives her a shivery feeling. She gets up quickly, swinging her legs off the bed in one movement and shaking her head hard to clear it, and then she walks about the flat, switching on all the lights and drawing the curtains. She has never liked to be in a room at night with the curtains undrawn, even when there is no possibility, or rather no rational possibility, of anyone looking in. Still, Mary feels herself observed and so makes sure no inch of window is left inadvertently uncovered.

She sits at the desk in her room, her chin in her hands, her elbows on the leather desk-top, staring into space. Sometimes she gets up and walks slowly through the flat, her property now, stopping before the convex mirror in the hall, before the wing mirror in the master bedroom, before the wall mirror in the bathroom. Her face looks back at her, white and blank. She examines it without interest, as she examines the other objects reflected there: the china plates and jugs in their glass cabinet in the hall, or the huge bed with its dark red counterpane in Phoebe's room.

Sometimes she sits in her armchair and knits, but she does not knit very much any more, the arthritis has got to her fingers. When Phoebe was alive it was possible for her to listen to her movements as she knitted, to know if she was asleep or looking through her old photographs or pottering about in her room. But now it is different. Now there is nothing to listen out for.

Sometimes, on her way back from the bathroom, Phoebe would stop at the door of Mary's room. If it was ajar she would push it open. If it was open she would step into the room. Mary would show her the flowers the girl had brought.

– That will brighten up the room, Phoebe would say. She herself could not stand the smell of flowers in her room. They gave her a headache. Besides, she would say, they are so messy.

Mary still sometimes goes to the cinema. As before, she often falls asleep as soon as the lights go out. She thinks, as she drifts off, of open doors and convex mirrors, of Phoebe in her bed under the dark red counterpane, or of the girl's big friend writing in his chair under the mirror. But she goes out less and less often. Most of the time she is content to wander through the flat. She will sit down at any point in these wanderings, on any chair, her expression unchanging, her thoughts flowing away from her. Minutes, or sometimes hours later, she finds herself sitting in the chair in the hall or at the kitchen table, and cannot remember how she got there.

As the film comes to an end she wakes up with a start. She has that capacity, to wake up at once the moment the film comes to an end.

In her room she arranges the flowers and puts them on the chest of drawers or on a corner of her desk. She looks forward to Saturdays and a fresh bunch.

In the hall the man is scribbling in his notebook, lips

pursed, forehead puckered. The pen flies over the white pages. His moving hand is reflected in the mirror.

In the master bedroom, behind the firmly shut door, the old lady is saying:

— I showed you his last letter, didn't I?

— Yes, the girl says.

The old lady pulls the contents out of her bag and strews them on the counterpane.

— You showed it to me, the girl says.

— Are you sure? The most recent one?

The letter is three years old. It is creased with age and going brown at the folds.

— I do hope he's done the right thing, the old lady says. Going out to those Eastern places.

The girl is reading the letter.

— He said he would be ever so careful, the old lady says. None of this would have happened if he hadn't been seduced from his marriage.

Mary sits at her desk, her head cupped in her hands, staring at nothing. Her door is ajar, as it always was, even though now the flat is empty. Sometimes she gets up and goes on a slow tour of inspection, stopping before a mirror or a window, sitting in the chair in the hall or the one beside the big bed in the master bedroom.

— Mary imagines I will leave all this to her when I pass on, the old lady says. What a funny idea. As if I owed her anything.

The niece is silent.

— I have decided to leave it to you and only to you, the old lady says.

— Please, Phoebe, the niece says. I don't want to hear about things like that.

– Why not? the old lady says. Why should we not face the facts as they are?

– I may well die before you, the niece says.

– You may, the old lady says. But it is highly unlikely.

Sometimes she will sit for hours in a chair that is not hers, not part of her room. Of course all that is in the flat is hers now, but she still cannot get used to the fact. She glides over the carpets in her slippers, making no sound. She tries to remember what her past was like, to ask herself what memories she still carries with her, but they seem more unreal even than the memories of other people.

She tries to imagine herself and Robert in – where was it Phoebe said? Amalfi? What does one do in Amalfi? In Rome? In Geneva?

She remembers without difficulty Phoebe at school, Phoebe at home, Phoebe's marriage, her own interview with Phoebe on her return to England, and then their life together here, in the flat.

– The truth is, Phoebe says, I was better off without him. I hoped someone would take him off my hands.

– Off your hands? Mary asks, surprised.

– In my family, Phoebe says, we pride ourselves on the fact that no one has ever been divorced. Few of the marriages, however, have been what you would call happy. It was time to get rid of Robert.

Mary looks through the stacks of photographs which Phoebe has left her, with the rest of the contents of the flat. But she cannot find the photo of the three of them together taken by Phoebe's cousin Freddy, with the house tilting slightly as though it were about to fall down on top of them, and Phoebe's right arm inexplicably missing and all of them except perhaps Phoebe herself blissfully unaware that anything was wrong.

— I felt it was time, Phoebe says. I needed to be alone. As one does. At certain moments of one's life.

— You could have gone away yourself, Mary says.

— I have never fancied being the guilty party, Phoebe says. If you go away you are automatically the guilty party.

And to the niece she says, behind the firmly shut door:

— Mind you, I can understand David perfectly. I too needed to be alone. I would never have been so vulgar and predictable though as to run away with someone else.

The niece is looking into the crown of her big straw hat.

— When she cannot look into my eyes, Phoebe says to Mary afterwards, that is what she does, she looks down into the crown of her big straw hat.

— I imagine he used this other woman as a stepping stone, Phoebe says.

The girl does not move.

— I mean, Phoebe says, to hop from his marriage into a comfortable bachelor existence. After all, he has everything he needs, a large flat, plenty of servants, an interesting job, a pleasant social life. Can you blame him?

The girl does not answer.

— Naturally, knowing what a chatterbox I am, the old lady says, he hesitates to confide in me. That is sad, but understandable.

— You have no idea then, the girl says, who it could have been he ran away with?

The old lady appears not to have heard.

— You have no idea? the girl repeats.

Mary, after the long climb up to the flat, stands for a moment in the entrance hall, her shopping bag in her hand. She listens for sounds of the old lady, straining her ears, then remembers that she is now alone in the flat and shakes her head a little as though to clear it.

In her room she lies on the bed, staring up at the ceiling, her face as expressionless as ever, her eyes wide open.

— I am not a leper, Phoebe had written in reply to her note. Come to tea at 4 on the second Friday of the month. And then, when she had come and they were sitting in Phoebe's bedroom:

— How would you like to help me run the flat?

— Run the flat?

— That's right.

— Meaning what exactly?

— It's too large for one. As you can see.

— Oh I don't think I could afford —

— That was not what I was suggesting, Phoebe had cut in quickly. You would help me run it and we would share what space there is. You would have your room. You could have a television set if you wished. And you would really have very little to do.

— If Mary thinks I am going to leave everything to her, Phoebe says loudly to the girl, then she has another think coming. Why should I leave anything at all to the woman who called herself my best friend and then cynically stole my husband?

— Shshshshsh! the niece says.

— Well, just tell me why I should?

— You can't make accusations like that, Phoebe, the girl says in an embarrassed whisper.

— I can speak the truth, can't I? We haven't yet reached

the stage where we are not allowed to speak the truth, have we?

— Oh, Phoebe! the girl says. Why do you say things like that? You only do it to tease!

— Well, I just want her to know she can't count on anything, Phoebe says.

— I'm sure she isn't expecting anything, the girl says.

Sometimes, after leaving the old lady, the girl comes into Mary's room, perches herself on the desk and chats. She tells Mary which films to see, which books to read.

— I've just finished a wonderful book. I don't know if it's your sort of thing. About an extraordinary man who fooled everyone that he was a Chinese scholar and a spy and the lover of the Empress of China. If you want I'll bring it round next week. A book about an amazing Welshman who sailed up into the Arctic Circle with only his dog and was marooned there for over a year and once a beam fell on him during a storm and knocked out his eye and it was hanging there by a vein or something and he just had to push it back into its socket and get on with things, I could hardly bear to read that bit. A book about hanging gardens and their history with wonderful pictures. A book about the pilgrim route to Santiago de Compostella. A book about miniature Eskimo sculpture. Actually most of their sculpture *is* miniature because they have so few stones and bones and things and such long nights in the winter and must make the most of what they have.

In the hall the man sits under the convex mirror, staring at the toe of his highly polished shoe. He has not moved since the girl went in to see the old lady. Sometimes he glances up and gazes down the long dark corridor. Then he returns to the contemplation of his shoe.

Mary stands at the window of the master bedroom, looking down into the gardens below. The room is bathed in a steady evening light. For a moment she has the sense of herself standing there, and of how she must look to someone else, someone who might be able to see her across the distance of the gardens, or perhaps someone who can fully imagine her as she stands, inside the room, her room now, one of the many rooms of what is now her flat, looking out.

VIII

And now at last I can speak.

I have wanted to once or twice before. When there was a pause in the conversation. Or I felt unhappy with the way something was said. But before I could take it the chance was gone. Now at last they have fallen silent and I can speak.

To say what?

I am here. In the flat. I move from room to room. The carpet mutes my steps. My face appears, white, in the mirror. I hold up my hand and it too, the palm of my hand, is white in the gathering darkness of the room. It is as if I were dead but also alive. My gaze is like water. It moves over the surface of that face, that hand, it spreads over the surface of the mirror. It is as though space were palpable and I could feel it. I am at the same time behind my eyes and the objects on which my eyes rest, including those eyes themselves, and that is strangely peaceful, as though I had come home after a long voyage, as though this were the destiny that had been waiting for me, that I had been awaiting.

Was it this I wanted to say? This for which I held myself back?

There is no sound. Even when the windows are open there is no sound. Even when it is night the light falls evenly.

Why am I here?

I talk to myself in the twilight. I sit in my room, at my desk, and I talk to myself. I murmur in the twilight. Sometimes I surprise them talking in the other room, her voice loud as she questions, bullies, argues, and the girl calming her, laughing at her, keeping up her spirits. I think in a moment I will open the door and enter into their midst, but I do not.

It is best in the middle of the day, in winter, when there is no sun but an even light, a light spread evenly through the whole flat. My feet make no sound on the carpet. I stand in the middle of the room in the even light. I walk from room to room. The windows are closed. There is no sound. I see this figure pass before me in the mirrors. I wake up and the impression is still vivid on my retina of this figure passing quickly yet without apparent hurry in front of all the mirrors, the convex and the winged and the fixed. I blink and rub my eyes but it takes a long time for the sensation to disappear.

Why am I here?

I see in my mind's eye the hall, the front door, the mirror, the chair. Sometimes I am sitting in the chair, in the hall. Sometimes I am writing in my notebook. Sometimes I am looking down the corridor into the lighted hall, sitting at my desk in the smaller of the two bedrooms, my head in my hands. I sit like that for hours. Then get up and wander through the empty flat. As I pass the mirrors a white face moves across the surface before me, in time to my steps. Fair hair. Am I still so young? After all that has happened?

But what is it exactly that has happened? That has

brought me here? Did she suspect? Or know? Was she saying something to me by leaving the place to me in the end?

It would have been only natural to leave it to Mary. After all those years together. I thought of stepping aside, of handing it over immediately to Mary, but she had gone. Had vanished. Leaving no address. And besides, if she did it that way there must have been a reason. Punishment or reward? Live on here and think about me. Think about what you did or did not do. Detach yourself slowly from all other entanglements and retreat into this flat. Walk through the rooms and think. Walk before the mirrors and wonder.

I lie on her bed and recall those days. I imagine the bell ringing on Saturday mornings and Mary's shuffling steps and the voices at the door and the flowers and the door to the bedroom opening and then the hours of conversation, one ear cocked to hear if anything was happening in the hall, the other bedroom, the kitchen, the bathroom, keeping the conversation going, mind on this betrayal and on that. In her room Mary sits and listens, turning over with one part of her mind the conversations of that morning or the previous week, trying to hear, to pick the words out of the quiet buzz, and the man, bent over his notebook, sucking his pen, occasionally looking up into the darkness of the corridor, or catching a phrase from the conversation in the closed room, his mind elsewhere, trying to concentrate, to shut out the other noises, to catch the elusive object always out of reach.

They are talking in there but the door is closed and nothing can be heard except the hum of voices, though it is possible, with an effort, to imagine what they are saying. In the hall, at the end of the corridor, I can see his form, his bulk. Sometimes he looks up, as if sensing that he is being watched, and our eyes meet, but he cannot really see into the darkness of the corridor and soon he drops his gaze. Sometimes the chair is empty. Sometimes I enter the big bedroom and we talk. At others I am lying on the immense bed with its red counterpane and letting my mind wander to her, the other, sitting at her desk, listening, waiting, waiting. I ask her sometimes what she is waiting for, whether she is waiting for me to die or to tell her I know all that has happened. But I do not tell her. I will not be the first to speak of these things. Perhaps they are not even true. But I think they are. The pieces fit. Everything is accounted for. Perhaps they fit too well. That is what occasionally worries me. Only an obsession would make all the pieces fit so well. Reality would be less tidy. But I do not think it is an obsession. I think it is the truth. But I will say nothing. Why should I say anything? Why should I tell her that I know? It is better like that, to keep her guessing, keep her wondering. She will not go so long as she does not know for certain that I too know. Not all the details, but the main lines, how they plotted and betrayed and fled and then fell out.

Sometimes I think of her sitting at her desk, the door ajar, peering through the crack, listening to all we say. I cease to pay attention to the other, the little one in here with me with her straw hat and her ash-blonde hair, and think only of her. Then I realize that I have been asked a question and that an answer is expected of me. Sometimes when she enters in a rush and pulls up the chair and sits, talking, giggling, exclaiming, I think of him sitting out there on the hard chair in the hall and wonder what he is doing. She assures me that he does not want to come in, is happier out there. I think of him as a bodyguard, a watchdog at the door. She tells me he is writing. I wonder if it is about us. Or about them. Perhaps he will give it to her when it is done and she will have to understand, reading it, what it is he cannot say directly. By the time she has finished reading he will be gone. Then all she will have of him is what she holds in her hands.

I would like to be alone. I would like the flat to be empty of all these people. There are too many of them. I think about them too much. But then I wonder if it isn't just because I am alone that I think so much about them, about her in the other room and the blonde one here and him, the watchdog by the door. It is so difficult to be alone if you are alone. It's not easy when someone else is there but it is a little easier than when there is no one. That is one of the sad laws of life.

The woman comes every day and brings the food and cleans the flat. She stays for the precise hour for which I pay her. Then she enters, without knocking, and says: 'The hour's up, Missis.' Then I thank her and pay her and she goes. Back to her husband. He can no longer move easy, she says. The rest of the time I am alone. I get up occasionally to go to the kitchen, the bathroom. On my way back I peer into the other rooms, or into the hall. The flat is empty. I like it like that and I do not like it like that. I am happy to have it that way and I am not happy to have it that way. Why do people never imagine that these two states, happiness and unhappiness, can co-exist?

I sometimes think I should have someone living in. The flat is big enough. There is a bedroom ready. I would not mind if they brought a television set, so long as the sound was kept low. Someone, a friend in need, to look after my own simple needs. That would have been good. Might still be. Occasionally I receive letters from old friends: 'Back in England at last. Would love to see you.' I never reply.

I pass through the flat, silently, in the even light. I do not stop in front of the mirrors, but I look as I pass and there is no reflection, however fleeting, to make me pause. That does not surprise me. That is what I was coming to. In fact it is a relief to be able to admit it. Though I pass and repass and sit and lie and stand and look and even remember and hear, there is no reflection as I pass. I know every corner of the flat, I have felt the softness and hardness of every chair, of every bed, I have looked from every angle and at every hour of the day and night. I am in total possession of it. It is there, waiting for me. It will always wait. It is empty. I am not alone in it. It is empty. I am here and yet it is empty. I possess it and yet it is uninhabited. It waits, like a flat seen in a mirror, silent, unchanging.

Where is it then?

In my memory? I do not think so.

I have memories, of course. No one is so poor that he does not. But why are mine so thin, so insubstantial, so lacking in flesh and blood, when in other respects I am not so very different from other people? Why do the inhabitants of this flat seem so much more real to me than my own memories? Why does my heart stir as I contemplate them, while the memories of my own life, my very own life, seem like a set of not very interesting and rather unlikely stories?

When I am asked I tell these stories. It seems to interest

other people. I cannot think why.

I have never understood why people write their memoirs, their autobiographies. Are their lives, their past lives, so solid then? And why, if they are, do they feel the need to recount them? Why does mine seem like nothing, or rather, like something for which there are no words and for which I feel no need to search for words?

Perhaps we cannot write about our real selves, our real lives, the lives we have really lived. They are not there to be written about. The conversation always goes on in another room. Or is that too easy?

I stop in front of the mirror in the bathroom and contemplate my face and see if I can find an answer there, but of course there is no reflection in the mirror. The flat is empty. I glide through the rooms. I pass effortlessly through walls, through skulls. Circulars have piled up on the carpet by the front door. No doubt sooner or later someone will enter. An estate agent, perhaps, to see what kind of property it is he has been asked to sell. Or the relatives to whom it has been left.

I need to go away from here. I need to go somewhere more real, somewhere I know better. The flat is beginning to grow insubstantial even as I talk. I am no longer even sure of its shape, of the way the rooms relate to each other. Sometimes the kitchen is at the end of the corridor, sometimes it is the bathroom that is there; sometimes the curtains are made of red velvet, sometimes of mere chintz; sometimes there are only two bedrooms and the hall, apart of course from the corridor, the bathroom and the kitchen, sometimes there is also a dining-room, though that is never used. Sometimes the flat is orientated east to west, sometimes north to south. And sometimes one room faces in one direction, sometimes in another.

It is quiet, here, now. I have no wish to leave. Besides, if I leave now, where shall I go? The places I once lived in will no longer receive me.

I have no wish to leave. But am I entitled to stay? It is as though so long as I was silent my presence passed unnoticed, but now I have spoken I have forfeited the right to stay.

But where will I go if I can no longer stay? As I listened to them, constrained to silence, I longed to be free. But it is impossible to live out in the open, with no doors and ceilings to protect you, no doors to shut out the wind, the noise.

Now I know that if I find another flat, another room, the pattern will repeat itself. So what am I to do?

Mary. She sits at her desk. The house is empty now. The flat. It belongs to her. As she knew it would. If she waited long enough. If she was patient enough. If she did not make a false move. Did not ask outright if the other knew. If she suspected. Sometimes she leaves her desk and walks aimlessly through the flat, to the kitchen, the bathroom, the hall, the other bedroom. She stands at the window, holding up the heavy curtains, looking down into the gardens. The windows are closed. They have always been closed. She stands in the even light of a winter afternoon, holding up the curtains with her left hand, looking out. Where has she come from? Out of what has she materialized?

I want to start again but it is too late.

I want to run to the end but where is the end?

Behind the doors, the murmur of conversation. In the depths of the corridor a door has been drawn open a few inches. One day there will be no conversation. There will be no eyes behind barely opened doors. The hall will be empty. The mirror reflect nothing. And then there will be no mirror, no furniture, only one empty room after another. And then no more rooms, no more house. As once there was none.

They may not have existed, the two young ones. Only been a game the old ones played. We'll ask Sal. Sal knows nothing. She's a modern girl. She lives buried in the past. What books has she brought you? What flowers?

The watchdog at the door.

Now I see Mary as she sits with her elbows on the table, her chin in her cupped hands, wondering about the past. They have played the game so often it has acquired a kind of reality. But perhaps there was no husband, no son, no Rome, no Amalfi, no air-conditioned flat in the Gulf. Perhaps there are only two old ladies slowly dying together in a cramped flat in West London.

She cannot think clearly for any length of time. At moments it seems to her that all these people have been here. Are here. In the flat. With her. She wakes up and there is the girl, blonde, excited: – Oh, Phoebe! she says, and laughs her rich high laugh. At other times she thinks she hears the door and calls out: – Is that you, Mary? and waits to see the familiar stocky figure silhouetted in the doorway. She cannot remember if they really exist, or existed, or whether she read about them somewhere or simply made them up to pass the time. Everything has got so confused recently. Once she knew where she was, could let her mind wander but summon back the present when she needed to. But for some time now that has no longer been possible. She walks through the flat in her bare feet, making no noise on the thick carpets, looking in all the mirrors but without seeing any reflection there, only the wall on the opposite side of the room. That is something she does not quite understand, has not quite fathomed. Is she losing her sight or is she losing her mind? She knows that somewhere, some time, she will understand. But not yet. Not yet. Was that my life? she wonders, and sighs.

Why do I persist in imagining her? What is she to me that I should go on in this way?

When such questions grow insistent it is time to stop. There will be a flurry, perhaps a last flourish, even a surprise, and then silence.

Afterwards, perhaps, I will start again.

I have failed. I tried to enter this flat, these people, and I failed. All I could do was slip in and out of rooms, of heads. What comfort is there in that? So I tried at last to break away, to speak in my own voice, of my own concerns, and relegate the flat and its inhabitants to the dustheap of the imagination. I have failed in that too. In my own voice I had nothing to say, and as for them, they refused to disappear.

I am beginning to see though that to talk of failure may be as misleading as to talk of success. I have tried, and now I know. I know it never stops, the murmur of conversation. You cannot stop it. You cannot hear with any clarity but you cannot altogether cease to hear. When you enter, when you push open the door and step in, then, for a moment, there is silence. You look round and there is no one there. And you go out and it starts again. You go to sleep and it is there. You wake up and it is there. It does not stop. You cannot stop it. Though there may be a pause, a momentary silence, it will always pick up again. Not here. But in another room. And another. And another.

Perhaps that is as it should be. To ask for more may be to ask for the impossible. Which will not be given.

IX

By now it is almost a ritual. The doorbell rings at 10.30 every Saturday morning and there on the landing is the niece with her man and a large bunch of flowers in her hand.

— I hate the word bouquet, she says to the old lady, once she is safely inside her room and the door has been shut.

— Bouquets belong to my girlhood, the old lady says.

— I just pick what I can find, the girl says.

— Mary doesn't know one flower from another anyway, the old lady says.

— I'm sure she does, the girl says. She loves flowers.

— Hearing you talk one would think it was she you were related to, not me, the old lady says.

— Oh, Phoebe! the girl says, I just think you're being a bit unfair.

— At my age, the old lady says, one is entitled to a little unfairness.

— One isn't at any age, the girl says.

— You're a Puritan, the old lady says. I don't know why you should be, your mother was anything but.

— I take after my father, the girl says.

The old lady does not appear to have heard.

— What did you think of him? the girl asks.

The old lady is hunting in her bag, which is lying next to her on the counterpane.

— What did you think of him? the girl asks again.

— Have you seen my handkerchief? the old lady asks. I can't seem to find it.

The girl takes the bag from her and pulls out the handkerchief.

— Thank you, the old lady says.

The girl waits.

— You *are* fierce this morning, the old lady says.

— Fierce? Me?

— I will tell you, the old lady says. I did not like him but I respected him.

— Why?

— Why did I respect him?

— No. Why didn't you like him?

— Those are mysteries, aren't they? the old lady says.

— Oh, Phoebe! the girl says.

— I don't know why I let her come, the old lady says to her companion when the girl and her friend have gone. She gushes and giggles more and more each time I see her.

— You put her off, Mary says. She doesn't know which way to turn.

— But I show nothing, the old lady says.

— Precisely, Mary says. She doesn't know where she stands with you. It makes her gush and giggle.

— But to that extent?

— It's kind of her to come, Mary says.

— Is it? the old lady asks. I would rather then that she took her kindness elsewhere.

— She is devoted to you, Mary says.

— You know very well why she comes to see me, the old

lady says. It is out of guilt. She cannot bear to live with
herself after what she did to David.

— You know that isn't true, Mary says.

— I have eyes, the old lady says. Now show me what
you bought for supper.

In her room Mary sits on the bed reading an old issue of
Films and Filming which the girl has brought her. But she
is restless. The silence oppresses her. She gets up and
opens the door, very quietly, a few inches.

In the corridor, between the door and the wall, under
the convex mirror, sits the niece's friend, gazing at the toe
of his well-polished shoe. He glances at his watch.

In her room the old lady says:

— One day she will confess to me. I am only waiting for
that day.

— Oh, Phoebe! the girl says.

— Yes, the old lady says. She thinks I don't know. She
thinks I never knew. Whereas I was actually relieved. I
was relieved to see the back of them. I could almost say I
willed it to happen.

The girl glances surreptitiously at her watch.

— If you want to go, go, the old lady says. But don't
sneak covert glances at your watch. You know I can't
bear that.

— No, no, the girl says, blushing violently. I don't have
to go for a little while yet.

— Is it the car again? the old lady asks.

— No, no, the girl says. We have to look in on a friend of
Mike's mother.

— I didn't know he had a mother, the old lady says.

— Oh, Phoebe! the girl says.

The old lady is silent.

– There's plenty of time, the girl says.

– Time for what? the old lady asks.

– Well, time for me to be with you.

– I am quite happy by myself, the old lady says. I don't want any favours done to me.

The girl is silent, looking down at the crown of her straw hat.

The old lady stretches out an arm and touches her. – I didn't mean to offend you, she says.

– Oh, Phoebe! the girl says.

– I wish you would try to find out about conditions in the Gulf though, the old lady says.

– I told you, the girl says. Everything's fine.

– But you haven't heard from him?

– How could I if you haven't?

– That doesn't follow, the old lady says. What would he want to write to me for?

– What would he want to write to *me* for then? the girl says.

– You were always close, the old lady says.

The girl shrugs.

– You know, the old lady says, I always secretly hoped it would be you he would marry.

The girl puts the straw hat down on the floor under her chair.

– It may happen yet, the old lady says. There may yet be a blessing in all this.

The girl gets up and goes to the window.

– I'm sure Michael is a very worthy person, the old lady says. But he's not really one of us, is he?

The girl is looking down into the gardens.

– I have the feeling that you are already tiring of him,

the old lady says. That if something were to happen now your whole life would change.

— Happen? the girl says. Like what?

— Well, the old lady says, if I died, for instance, and left you the flat.

— Oh, Phoebe! the girl says. Don't talk like that.

— Well, it's bound to happen sooner or later, isn't it? the old lady says.

— You'll outlive us all, the girl says.

The old lady laughs.

The girl returns and sits again at the head of the bed, in the chair she has just vacated.

— It could happen, of course, the old lady says. But it wouldn't be much fun for me then, would it?

— I don't know, the girl says. You'd get by. You'd find ways of amusing yourself.

— I could tell myself stories, the old lady says.

Something about her tone makes the girl look up. — Oh, Phoebe! she says.

The old lady is not looking at her. She has lain back on the pillows and is gazing up at the ceiling.

The girl is silent. Finally the old lady says:

— Something is going to happen. I feel that something is about to happen.

The girl is silent. But when it is clear that the old lady has nothing more to say she asks:

— Something? Like what?

— It was just a passing thought, the old lady says. I doubt if anything will happen now.

In the hall Mike takes a notebook from one pocket of his jacket and a pen from another, lays the notebook on the arm of the chair, bites his lower lip and begins to write.

— The autumn always does this to me, the old lady says. It makes me feel most peculiar.

The girl does not answer.

— Not you? the old lady asks.

— But autumn's been over for ages, the girl says. It's practically spring now.

— It's approaching again, though, the old lady says. I can feel it approaching.

The girl is silent.

— I imagined you didn't exist, the old lady says.

The girl laughs uncertainly.

— I woke up, the old lady says. It was all confused.

— Oh, Phoebe! the girl says.

In the hall Mike is scribbling in his notebook, his pen racing over the page. His moving hand is reflected in the convex mirror.

The girl says nothing.

— And Mary hardly helps, the old lady says. She's even more muddled than I am.

— Is she? the girl says.

— I called her in the middle of the night, the old lady says. My chest was hurting and I called her. And she came running in in her dressing-gown with her shopping bag in her hand. If that isn't being muddled, what is?

— She was going out shopping?

— I don't know what she was doing, the old lady says. I told her it was the middle of the night and I had only called her because of this pain in my chest.

— In your chest? What kind of pain?

— I thought it was the end, the old lady says.

— You didn't call a doctor?

– What would a doctor do? the old lady says. If it's time for me to go I'll go and that's that.

– Don't talk like that, Phoebe, the girl says.

– Why not? the old lady says. To spare your feelings?

– No, the girl says. Just – don't.

The old lady does not appear to have heard. The girl looks out of the window, twirling her straw hat in her hand.

– Everybody stops all of a sudden, the old lady says.

– Stops? What do you mean?

– I mean what I say. I just have the feeling that everything stops. Then it goes on again. It's a little uncanny.

Outside, in the hall, Mike lays his notebook and pen on the chair as he gets up. He stretches, then walks slowly round the little entrance hall, looking intently at each of the three pictures, the watercolour, the portrait and the print, then bends and looks at the few pieces of china displayed in the little glass corner cabinet.

In her room Mary sits motionless behind her desk, door ajar in front of her. In the convex mirror in the hall at the end of the corridor can be seen the notebook and pen lying on the chair, but the hall now appears to be empty. Then the man appears in one corner, approaches the chair, picks up the notebook and pen and sits again.

He sucks the pen, his eyes closed. Then he bends again and starts to write.

The girl is getting up. She is still talking to the old lady, but she has got up. She is moving towards the door. Now the door opens and in the hall the man stands up. In the mirror it is possible to see the door opening, to see the girl in her white summer dress and wide-brimmed straw hat stepping out of the room, to see the man taking a stride towards her. The door is quite open now and it is possible to see, in the convex mirror, the girl advancing towards the large young man who himself moves forward to meet her, and, behind them, in the room, sitting up in the immense bed, her hands pressing against her ears, her mouth open, the old lady. Is she screaming? Is she about to fall back on the bed in a dead faint? Is this why the young man has rushed forward and the girl has half-turned, at the door, shrinking up to him but turning her face back towards the room? Or is the old lady merely saying goodbye to them?

It is impossible to say, for no sound emerges from any of them.

It is possible to see all this in the convex mirror, from the rooms along the corridor. But though the door of one of the rooms is ajar there is no one to see it. Mary, in this room, is asleep with her head on the desk. Or perhaps it is something more than sleep, for she does not move at all as she lies slumped there, her head on her arm, her hand open on the desk, the other arm dangling down to the floor.

There is no one to see her in this position, and she herself has ceased to see. Or perhaps even this is merely one more image that flashes through her mind as she lies, fitfully sleeping, on her bed, one more image of the large young man and the golden-haired girl in the big straw hat and the old lady sitting up in bed, her hands pressed to her ears, her mouth open, in the room beyond.

Perhaps the mirror does not register this scene at all, as the girl half cries out and the man holds her, in the doorway of the room, and both look back, from the hall, into the bedroom from which the girl has just emerged.